Tony Needs Speed

STEELTOWN CHRONICLES, Volume 4

Dave Walker

Published by Dave Walker, 2025.

TONY NEEDS SPEED

First edition. July 24, 2025.

ISBN: 978-1069682833

Written by Dave Walker.

Also by Dave Walker

Watch for more at www.davewalkerauthor.com.

For anyone who ever had to let go of the past to move into their future.

Special thanks to motorsport writer Tim Miller of *The Hamilton Spectator* for his expert advice and endless patience dealing with my newb questions.

And, of course, thanks to Anne, for her endless help and encouragement!

"So on we go

His welfare is of my concern

No burden is he to bear

We'll get there"

--The Hollies, "He Ain't Heavy, He's My Brother"

"I've been waiting so long to sing my song."

--Alice Cooper, "Hello, Hooray"

Chapter 1

THURSDAY, AUGUST 4, 2005, 9:00 a.m.

My skin crawled. I hated this memory. After Frankie had been born, I'd taught myself to *forget*.

But now for some reason I couldn't. Once again, I was that scared seven-year-old peering out of his bedroom window, watching his dad's gangster buddies, Beppe Santucci and Uncle Toto, drive up in their black '59 Cadillac Fleetwood, about to steal Dad away from us.

I glanced nervously around the Rockford Raceway, half-expecting to see them.

Then I told the memory to go fuck itself. But this particular memory had attitude.

Angie and I were half-way up in the stands, wearing our old, jean jackets—Canadian Tuxedos—waiting to cheer on Angel, at the Junior Go-Kart Mark IV Ontario Championship race. At ten years old, our daughter was currently ranked second in Ontario. She was a prodigy, like her old man had been. Today, she was competing against fourteen other Karters. Ranked first was hotshot Max Ciprietti, the kid to beat.

The raceway was twenty-eight kilometers northwest of Hamilton, along Highway 8.

Rockford was known for sprint car racing, mini-stocks, and Thunder Stocks. Last year, they'd hosted the Southern Ontario Sprint Car Nationals, which was a big deal.

If my little Angel won today, she'd go to Barrie for the Canadian Championships. Win that, and she'd represent Canada at the World's in California. So, the pressure was intense. I was doing my best to appear calm, but, dammit, I really wanted to her to win.

Hey, asshole, you shouldn't have quit racing! What kind of example is that for your kid? Coward!

I plowed that shithead demon back into its cage. It always showed up at the worst times.

We'd arrived early in the pick-up truck to unload her kart and grab good seats. Karting was gaining in popularity. Parents forked out big bucks on expensive rigs and track time and private coaching, all to give their kids an edge. Lucky for us, Angel was a natural, and since I was her mechanic, money wasn't much of an issue.

Standing on the track apron, wearing a red-and-white racing suit, she was talking shop with the other drivers like a little grown-up. I couldn't have been more proud of her. She'd had the confidence I'd had at her age. And I was relieved she was a happy extrovert like her mom, not a brooder like me, Mr. Leather Heart. I had no idea what my wife Angie saw in me. I've always thought I looked like a mean old bulldog. But it seems like she'd made it her life's mission to penetrate that tough heart of mine.

The buzz of excitement today was nothing like I'd felt in my teens and early twenties, racing micro sprints. But when I'd become a dad at twenty-one, I'd quit cold turkey. Unlike *my* old man, I'd vowed to be a *good* one. So far, I hadn't let myself down, and I didn't plan to. Being a good dad was the most important job I'd ever have.

Angie and I squeezed hands. Then she planted a wet one on my cheek. How lucky was I?

An hour later, under a cool blue sky, the drivers ran their karts through the pace lap. A warm breeze sailed through the tall chain link fence and up into the packed stands.

I was relieved to see that my Angel was easily as good as Ciprietti. Her *Birel Art* GoKart was in top shape, thanks to yours truly. I'd spent all week in the garage, going over it with a fine-tooth comb. I'd tightened up the bolts, replaced the chain and brake pads, bled the brakes, welded a crack in the frame, checked the clips on the kingpins and tie rods, dumped in a new battery, oiled and greased all the moving parts, and tuned the engine to perfection. When it came to engines, I was the King. I'd never met a motor I couldn't successfully smooth-talk. It was relationships with humans that gave me a headache.

The pace laps ended.

The karts lined up at the pole.

The fans were on their feet, cheering.

"You can do this!" Angie shrieked.

"You got this, Angel!" I shouted, my adrenaline pumping. I shot her our special two-thumbs up.

She waved up at us, beaming, and returned the gesture.

I was so proud of her. I wiped a single tear from my eye, as discreetly as I could, though Angie caught the play and squeezed my waist.

The green flag dropped. The karts thundered off. The crowd roared as their kids jockeyed for position. I bellowed with the best of 'em.

"You're like a big kid when you watch Angelina race," Angie said in my ear.

We shared a quick, hot kiss

"The luckiest kid," I said, pulling away.

This was a twenty-lap race. We were on the edge of our seats the whole time. Half way through lap fifteen, Angel edged past Max and took the lead!

I fist-pumped the air.

Now she was two car lengths ahead of Ciprietti. Holy shit! And she was swinging through the front straight into her final lap!

Angie and I shouted until our throats hurt.

Ciprietti was slowly gaining, but not fast enough to pass my girl. She'd never lost a race when she was that far ahead and that close to the finish line. She was definitely going to win!

Then, like a slow-moving nightmare where you're trying to run from something evil, but you can't because your legs weigh a thousand pounds, everything changed.

Angel's car sputtered out.

"What the hell!" I roared. "There's no frickin' way!"

Heads turned. People tittered with sympathy.

Angel slid her kart off onto the grass just before the last turn. She threw up her hands with frustration and looked pleadingly towards us in the stands.

My heart broke for my little girl!

Angie wrapped her arm around me.

"I went over that kart with a fine-tooth comb. Someone fucked with our daughter's engine!"

Then I found myself thinking back to early that morning, when I'd been in the garage loading Angel's kart into my truck. I'd noticed the side door of the garage was unlocked, the same one John had recently forced open to steal my Camaro. Long story.

We were all very cautious to keep the place locked up. I had a lot of expensive tools. Nothing had seemed to be missing from the garage. Maybe it was time to install a security camera.

I blinked myself back to reality.

Suddenly, I was feeling that the air wouldn't go into my damn lungs. Panicked, I gasped and clutched my chest.

Distraught, Angie grabbed my shoulder. "Tone, what's wrong? Are you having a heart attack?"

The sense of something magnetic and evil had rotated my gaze towards the far end of the bleachers. Oh God, it felt so much like that damn memory.

Leaning against the far rail of the stands, in a white t-shirt, black jeans, and a black fedora was a pale, doughy young man. He was chomping on gum, sneering at me. His face was cold. And somehow familiar.

My legs wobbled. I dropped against the seat.

"Tone, seriously, what's wrong?"

"They're fucking with me again."

"Who's fucking with you?" Angie's head jerked around.

And when she spotted him, too, I could tell she was as freaked out as I was.

Chapter 2

THAT NIGHT, AFTER DINNER, I did something I'd never done before—I called an emergency meeting at Tim Horton's. How desperate was I?

The usual Saturday night misfits and losers were there, killing time, as we hung at our table next to the window.

Donny had been trying to convince Norb and John that we should find investors and make a movie called *The Village Idiots*, a comedy about four guys from Ontario who play street hockey and somehow, against all odds, make it to the World Ball Hockey finals. As if anyone would bother going to a movie like that!

"Enough with the friggin' pipe dreams, Love," I grumbled.

Donny laughed. "So, what's got you so cheesed off? You never call a meeting. Did Angela threaten to divorce you?" He winked at the others to show how funny he thought he was.

The words puked out of me like hot oil from a blown gasket. "Some wop piece of shit sabotaged Angelina's kart today at the track. She would have won!"

I slammed my fist against the table and sloshed coffee out of cups. "No one fucks with my daughter and gets away with it! No one!"

The whole place went silent, then quickly built up steam again. In the Hammer, an angry rant was no big deal.

I don't think my friends had ever seen me this mad. I couldn't remember *being* this mad, even when the Leafs lost to the Philadelphia Flyers in the Conference Semifinals.

Norb kept nervously eyeing the window beside him, maybe trying to decide if he should escape through it. Norb wasn't good with people in a rage.

I felt shitty that I'd scared him. That was the last thing he needed, after everything he'd gone through with The Screw and Mutti.

I made myself take a deep breath.

"Sorry, Norb. Sorry, boys."

"No worries, Tone," Norb squeaked. He looked at John and Donny for reassurance.

Donny looked blasé, but John had narrowed his eyes and was doing his best impression of an x-ray machine on me.

"I'm worried about you, Tone," Norb said. "We all are."

"I'm alright but what about my kid? Angelina's been crying all friggin' day. She's totally devastated."

I could tell my buds were eager to hear more so they could help me, but that was never going to happen. I usually came here to escape my problems by listening to how much worse their lives were. I didn't usually vent—that was their jam.

I thought of myself as a tough-minded family man who didn't air his personal shit, especially in a coffee shop. I would take care of business on my own, like a man.

Besides, they were the Village headcases, not me. I was the rock. The Dad-figure. The *Listener*. Yet, here I was tonight, whining and fussing like a baby. It was seriously unsettling to me.

Angie had encouraged me to hang with my friends to help take my mind off of this horrible day and the piece-of-shit Doughboy in the stands. By the time I'd collected myself enough to confront the guy, he'd vanished. At least Angie had seen him, too, so I knew I wasn't crazy.

Norb's open-mouthed chewing had hypnotized me. Lately, he'd gotten worse. Bits of sprinkle donut fell out of his mouth like soggy fireworks.

"Oh, my gawd, Tony," he said, "poor little Angelina! No wonder you called a meeting. And you *never* call a meeting."

"Yes, it's usually one of us losers who do that," John said, with a wry smile. Since marrying Sheena, he wasn't nearly as sarcastic or bitter. And we were all happy about that. Everyone'd had enough of the old John.

But I *was* happy he was no longer depressed or suicidal. I had no idea if he and Donny were each still on meds or getting counselling, but they both seemed pretty healthy. Besides, it was none of my business. I cursed myself for calling the guys together. My problems were mine.

"This is my first and last meeting," I grumped. "Trust me."

But shivers crept up my spine and buzzed at the base of my neck, when I thought of the cold-eyed Doughboy sneering at me.

I'd originally planned to stay for an hour at most, get the boys to talk about themselves, then hit the road before the conversation turned to me. Well, that plan had gone to shit, hadn't it?

"Why would someone fuck with Angelina's Kart?" Donny asked. "It's a kid's sport. Not exactly Nascar with a huge cash prize at stake. Is there a cash prize?"

"Nah, only trophies," I said.

A damn burst inside me. I was disappointed in myself, but I was also desperate—I told them the entire story. "And I'm pretty sure that psycho Doughboy broke into my garage and dumped sand in the gas tank."

"Why would he do that?" Donny asked doubtfully. "Nice villain name, by the way. Doughboy. Sounds like a Gotham City maniac. Bakes Batman and Robin inside a giant crescent roll."

Norb grinned excitedly, then remembered that we were here for real-life problems.

I glared at Donny. "That's what *I* call him. Although I should talk. I'm not exactly the poster boy for fitness."

"Doughboy might be dangerous, despite his name," Norb warned.

"He obviously didn't want Angelina to win," I said. "He had no problem fucking up an innocent little girl. What if she crashed? She coulda been hurt!"

"Who exactly is this Doughboy?" John asked.

"Don't know. But he's definitely a wop. A bad one."

Norb's face flushed—he hated it when I used the "w" word.

"Think he's Mafia?" Donny asked. He sounded intrigued.

"Doubt it," I scoffed. Why did non-Italians always assume the Mob was to blame? I forced down the old memory, feeling uneasy.

"Did you call the cops?" John asked.

I scowled at my friends. "No frickin' way."

"Why not?" Norb asked softly. "I would, if someone dumped sand in my daughter's gas tank and ruined her chances of winning. That's as bad as stealing cookies from a Girl Guide and ruining her chances of getting a Participation Certificate."

"Yep, just as bad," said John, biting his lip to keep from laughing at Norb. He was trying these days, I'd give him that.

"You don't understand, Norb," I growled.

"So how about you *make* us understand Tony?" Donny asked

Normally, I would have told Donny to shove it, but there was too much at stake. I lowered my voice. "I think someone's trying to send me a message."

"At a kid's go-kart race?" John said.

"Who'd even care about kids in go-karts, anyway?" Donny laughed.

I shot him a death-stare. Norb and John looked nervous, as if I might really kill Donny. Donny just smirked.

"What kind of message?" Norb whispered.

For once, *I* was the center of attention. And my buddies knew how much I hated that, how I was happiest on the sideline, throwing in my two cents to help them overcome their fucked-up-ness. How was it my turn? *I* was the fucked up one!

And no matter how hard I tried to stay in front of them tonight, I couldn't. It was harder than trying to tighten stripped screw heads.

"There's stuff about me you guys'll never know," I blurted. "And that's all I gotta say. End of story!"

Norb gasped. "Woah! Geez, Tony, stuff we'll never know? That sounds so mysterious, and *heavy*."

John just cocked an eyebrow at me.

"Don't sweat it, Tony," Donny said. "Everyone's got skeletons in their closet."

"Some more than others," John ribbed him, despite himself. Sighing, he crossed his legs and bobbed his pointy shoe faster than usual. He stared at his coffee cup. I figured this was John working hard at not saying anything more that he'd be ashamed of. Although I was glad he was nicer now, I kinda missed the old, sharp-tongued John. Still, change was good.

My friends stared at me, obviously hoping I'd spill the beans. Dammit, why had I ever opened my big mouth? I'd broken my own rule.

I was about to tell them to knock it off, when the coffee shop door was flung open, wind gusting in.

We all turned our heads.

My heart drummed a fucked-up beat, the old bad feeling yowling inside me.

His head looked like it had been squished in a vise. The skin of his face stretched tightly over sharp bones. His eyes were hawkish and piercing and even his old brown suit and gold tie couldn't soften the menace of the man. Uncle Toto was just as creepy as I remembered him.

Chapter 3

THE MAN I'D BEEN TAUGHT to call Uncle Toto was sitting beside me in the back seat of a gunmetal grey Ford Windstar, grinning cockily.

Gone was the menacing Cadillac Fleetwood.

I hadn't seen Toto and the other asshole since I was eleven, when they'd stopped coming around the house. I'd just hoped they were dead by now, or retired, or whatever old, creepy mobsters did.

Toto wasn't actually my uncle, thank God. My Dad had tried to make him seem harmless to me and my sister Giuseppine, who we called Josie. But our guts had known Dad was lying.

Toto was bad, and whenever Ma saw him at the door, her eyes would boil with rage.

Toto Berlusconi was Dad's childhood buddy from the old country. Newly immigrated, Dad bumped into him downtown one day at the Little Italy Sports Club, and they'd become fast friends again.

Ma and Dad had first met at the Italian Club on Murray Street in 1957. It was love at first sight, Ma always told us, and they were married a year later. One night at a dance, Dad had introduced Toto to Ma. She'd taken an instant dislike to him and told Dad to stay away from that greasy "*pieno di merda!*"

Toto stopped coming to our door and waited for Dad outside in the Cadillac with Beppe. My mother's wrath was too much, even for him.

Dad always lied about where Toto and Beppe were taking him. Rabbit-hunting, eel-fishing, you name it, but Ma always called him out on his bullshit. No way any of those guys had stepped foot in the great outdoors. Even I'd known Dad was lying. When I was twelve, Josie told me she was convinced Dad had a mistress. Confused, I thought she meant our father worked as a butler, but when she told me what it meant I got really scared, then really angry. When Josie had asked our mother if she'd divorce Dad, Ma had freaked out and told Josie to mind her own business. So we both did our best to shut it all out. But our teen years were not happy ones, and we both struggled with hot tempers and bitterness.

When Toto had silently motioned with his head for me to follow him out to the minivan, I'd felt hypnotized, the way Norb did watching Karl perform a magic trick.

To me, Toto was still terrifying to look at. Some guys are just born creepy, I thought. No wonder I'd been scared of him as a kid. And I was scared of him now, noting a bulge inside his jacket pocket. But if I hadn't thought he was packing, I would have punched him in the head for all the years he'd fucked with my family.

I'd wanted to yell, "Speak your garbage, then let me go!" but I couldn't. The vibe in this minivan was ominous. Childhood fears knotted in my gut like scarves in a clothes dryer.

Toto cracked the window and blew out cigar smoke. A few cars were huddled in the parking lot in front of the Price Chopper next door, twilight in full swing.

Marvin, the Canadian Tire sausage man, was closing up his cart for the night.

I couldn't see the driver's face. He was staring out the window. In the passenger seat beside him was a very large man, still as a corpse.

I swallowed nervously. At least my friends knew where I was. Good old Norb was staring out the window, phone in hand, ready to dial 911 if he had to.

My door opened and Dad squeezed in beside me.

We hadn't spoken since Christmas, unless you call silence speaking. If he asked me anything I'd basically grunt, shrug, or leave the room, or mood block him. Needless to say, he stopped trying. Sometimes, my *heart* wanted to forgive him, but *I* didn't. The battle was ongoing.

He wouldn't look me in the eyes. He was ashamed of something, I could tell. I wasn't shocked to see him here with his gangster cronies.

Once a piece of shit always a piece of shit. I was so mad I wanted to spit in his face.

Toto's hot glare was getting on my nerves. I glared back at him, but I couldn't stop trembling. Then he blew smoke across gold-capped teeth into my face.

You win, asshole! Coughing my head off, I stared through the front windshield and crossed my arms against my chest. The smoke and heat and stress turned my stomach into a bowl of rancid wine grapes.

I glared at Uncle Toto and my dad with as much anger and hatred as I could muster. Toto seemed like the kind of guy who strangled people with piano wire. He was as much responsible for my unhappy childhood as my father, but I was now a grown-up man, not a kid.

Once I knew what they wanted, I'd fire them both the *ombrello* and hit the road!

The corpse grunted, reminding me how outnumbered I was.

"Hey buddy! You in the front seat," I cried, trembling. "Show your face, asshole!"

On a stiff, ancient neck, a giant head turned into the dim glow of the dome light.

Shock buzzed through me. Beppe Santucci? The Big Fat Wop himself? *The Number One Piece-of-Shit Mobster?* The prick who'd scared the crap out of me as a kid?

He'd aged. He looked like he'd had too many face lifts, and I thought of Wayne Newton. His face was so tight, I swear it was about to pop. And with his velour track suit and dyed black hair, he couldn't have looked more ridiculous. But his expression was still lethal. This was not a man you'd laugh at.

He threw Dad a kill stare. "What, you can't speak?"

Beppe looked away and shook his head with disgust. "A man who doesn't spend time with his family can never be a real man."

What the frig? The guy was quoting Don Corleone? Besides, it was like the pot calling the kettle black. In my opinion, none of these mafia dirtbags were real men.

Like a dutiful soldier, Dad raised his head and slowly met his commanding officer's gaze. He looked wickedly guilty.

"Talk Dad," I said, grimly, "Get this over with. Whatever the fuck *this* is."

Beppe nudged his driver, and suddenly we were driving, out past the Dollar Store into the heavy traffic, then north along Molson Boulevard.

"Where the fuck are we going?" *Shit!* I was going to die! I prayed that Norb had started his call to the police.

"*Shhhhhhhh*," Uncle Toto hissed, pressing his index finger to his mouth.

"No fuckin' way. *You* shush!" I was going to die, anyway. What did manners matter at this point?

His glared chilled me, but I didn't let on. I was sure they were going to fit me with lead boots and dump me into the Bay. I hope John had caught our license plate.

Beppe spun the radio dial and hit on an oldies AM station. Dean Martin was singing "Everybody Loves Somebody." Beppe sang along, painfully off-key, as the song put him in a cheery mood. This was one sick joke.

The driver reached down under his seat, lifted out a black fedora and stuck it on his head. He snickered at me in the rearview mirror. It was Doughboy!

"Sorry about the sand in your kid's gas tank," he said, way more sarcastically than John ever could, his accent straight-up mafia. "But I got your attention, didn't I?"

My rage quick-boiled. "Fuck you, punk! If you come anywhere near my daughter again, I'll rip out your lungs!"

I raised my hand to slap him, when Beppe beat me to it. He delivered a swift, swinging backhand against his cheek.

In shock, Doughboy lost control of the van and we veered towards oncoming traffic. At the last second, he jerked the vehicle back into our lane. He looked over at his boss like a frightened kid caught with his finger in a Nutella jar.

"You know the code!" Beppe snapped. "Kids are off-limits! I tole you a thousand times, Elio!"

"I'm sorry, Boss! Geez!" He massaged his cheek. In a pathetic attempt to save face, he sat taller and toughened up his expression.

"Dad," I snapped. "Speak. Now!"

"Soon, Tony," he said, softly. "We're almost there." He still wouldn't look me in the eye.

I was afraid to know where *there* was. Surely, my own father wouldn't sit by and let some mobsters kill me? As hardened against him as I'd become, the thought that he might do just that brought tears to my eyes.

Uncle Toto made a show of slipping his hand inside his jacket. Pretty sure it was on his gun.

Despite my fear, I eye-rolled him. I was pretty pissed off, too. I hadn't planned on my life ending this soon.

Doughboy veered east on Flux and drove the speed limit. *Is this how gangsters roll now?* Slowly? *In a minivan?*

"In the olden days," Beppe said hoarsely. "We tooled around in our Caddy, to show this town who was in charge. But a Windstar has more seating."

Toto and Doughboy snickered quietly.

Fuck off!

"The Windstar's pretty comfortable," Beppe said, "and the sound system is stellar. Good on gas, roomy, too. Makes me feel like I fit in with the rest of society. And you know how us Italians like to fit in."

More snickering from Toto and Doughboy.

"Plus, at my age," Beppe said, "who needs negative attention, *right*, Elio?" Beppe gave him a look.

"You got it, Boss," Doughboy said.

Beppe's eyes blazed with rage. "Stop with the 'boss' shit! No one says *Boss* anymore. And another thing, Elio, lose the fedora. It makes you look *stoopid*." He slapped the back of his hand against his palm not far from Doughboy's face, making him flinch. "No more attention-seeking, got it? Why do you think we're driving a fucking Windstar?"

"Sorry, Beppe," Doughboy said, and removed his hat.

Uncle Toto was tapping the thing under his jacket, his expression growing colder and steelier.

Sure, he was scaring me, but he was also royally pissing me off. Who the fuck did he think he was? If someone didn't tell me what was going on soon, I'd grab his gun and pop a cap in *his* skull! Might as well go down with a fight.

When we turned a corner, I choked up. We were on *my* street!

Two houses from mine, Doughboy edged the van against the curb and idled.

"Look, whatever this is," I pleaded, "leave my family out of it."

Beppe turned down the music.

Stiff-necked, he turned and faced Dad. "Frank, you speak now."

Swallowing, Dad faced me. He looked like Pinocchio ashamed of his growing nose.

For the first time since I was a teen, I locked gazes with my father. It was weird but familiar.

He'd aged since Christmas. He was obviously hurting. His own fault, of course.

I steeled myself. "Say what you gotta say, so I can go home and be the good family man *you* never were."

His face sank.

I clenched my teeth, preparing for the worst.

He spoke softly, calmly. "I'm so sorry, Tony, but Mr. Santucci has called in the chips on my old gambling debt. Four Hundred thousand."

My guts unravelled. My breathing accelerated. "Are you serious? How many years did it take you to screw over your family like this? Huh?"

"Twenty-five years."

"Twenty-five years?"

"It's a long story."

"Isn't it always!" I bellowed. "My goddam father!"

By the look on the mobsters' faces, I knew not to ask about it. If they put sand in Angel's gas tank, and her just a kid, what would they do to me, a grown-ass adult?

"Are you asking *me* for the money, Dad? Because if you are, you're out of luck. All my money is tied up in college tuition and mortgage payments."

"I'm not asking," he said quietly. At least he had the decency to look ashamed. "The *family* is. Do them a favour and the debt will be forgiven."

My stomach curdled. What about *our* family? Did we mean nothing to him?

I swallowed the hot lump in my throat. The grim determination on the faces of Toto, Beppe and Doughboy made me queasy.

"What?" I said, "You want me to break somebody's legs?"

Silence.

"Kill somebody? Rob a bank!" I tried to ignore the trembling in my legs.

Beppe gestured to an imaginary audience. "There is nothing either good or bad, but thinking makes it so."

What the hell? If I hadn't been so scared, I might have laughed. This guy thought he was freakin' Shakespeare or something!

"Tony," he said. His voice was suddenly very hoarse and papery, his accent super thick. "Do the organization a favour. Set your dad free."

I was freaking out. I was sure they wanted me to kill someone. This was all too much. It would have to be something pretty big for Beppe to forgive such a huge debt.

"My son's a famous sprint car racer," he said. "He's very, very good, but not good enough. He just needs a great mechanic, like you, and not only that, Tony Valentini, but you're the Prodigy, a mini-stock legend, so you know how to win."

I think my jaw might have dropped.

Beppe raised his palms like a priest invoking a blessing. "Tony, you make my Giorgio win the Canadian Sprint Car Nationals at Hermonville Raceway on September twenty-fourth and your father's debt vanishes." He puffed the debt away with a breath.

"You scared, Tony?" Toto said, the overhead light winking in a single gold tooth. He'd finally spoken. Weasel.

"Not scared of *you*." But damn right I was.

"What's your son's name?" I asked Beppe. Shit, I was going to do this, wasn't I?

"Giorgio."

My heart skipped a beat. "Giorgio Santucci? *The* Giorgio Santucci? The Ontario Sprint Car Legend? The *Second Place Slider?*" That was his nickname. I'd been following him for years in the *Hamilton Mountain News* and *Ontario Race Weekly*.

"Second, sure, but *never* first, Tony." Beppe leaned closer to me. He was practically out of his seat. "You *make* him come in first. If not, Pops pays me the same day. Cash." His face was getting red and tight. "Or, we go to Plan B. And you don't wanna know about Plan B. Right, Frank?"

"Yes, Don Beppe," Dad said. "Of course."

Dad's allegiance to this piece-of-shit sickened me.

Uncle Toto slid a handgun out of his pocket and rested it on his lap.

So he *did* have a gun!

He flexed his bony fist. Totally mobster.

"Look, I can't *make* a driver win," I said. "I can build and fine-tune a car, but the driver has to have the magic." I realized I'd been doing the finger purse, not a good idea with this guy.

Beppe shot me the dreaded chin flick. "Fuhgeddaboudit! *Make* him win or I bankrupt your Mama and Papa. Capeesh, you little shitball?" Straight-up psycho Wayne Newton.

Fear and rage were practically blowing steam out my ass. If there was one thing I hated, it was some asshole telling me what to do. This extortion was gonna kill me.

Dad, the coward, wouldn't look at me. "Do it for Ma, Tony," he whispered. "Please."

Beppe handed me a business card.

Randy R, Mechanic.

"Your new pit partner," he said. "He's *eccentrico*, but *genio*. Tomorrow morning, nine-o-clock. sharp. He's expecting you."

The silence in the car went pre-nuclear.

An eccentric genius, huh? Donny had once referred to himself that way and I'd almost puked.

Suddenly, Angie opened the front door of our house, pulled flyers out from the red mailbox, and slipped back inside. Thank God she hadn't noticed us.

But, here in the Windstar, all eyes were on me.

I was stuck between a rock and a hard place and there was only one way out.

"OK, I'll *make* him win, Mr. Santucci." I prayed I could actually deliver on that.

Beppe nodded at me, then turned stiffly around and slid a cassette into the stereo. He crooned along with Frank Sinatra's "My Way". What an ego.

Uncle Toto gestured for me to get out.

Dazed, I climbed past Dad, and slid the door shut. The van tore away from the curb.

Next door, the Smith's dog started yapping.

I bent over, elbows on my knees, gasping. Panic was pile-driving me. I had to achieve the impossible. As I began walking home, I stepped in dogshit.

Chapter 4

SUNDAY, AUGUST 7, 9 a.m.

As soon as I stepped outside of my car the dead-fish stink assaulted my nostrils. The wind was blowing it off Lake Ontario. Lucky me.

Randy's house was on the southern tip of Beach Boulevard, along the shoreline of Lake Ontario. The beach strip's hey-day had long since passed. But, in the last ten years, gentrification had made something of it. Rich people's dream homes now outnumbered the old cottages.

Still, some of the crappier houses had bars on their windows, like the one in front me.

Criminals afraid of other criminals breaking in, I thought, *and probably with good reason. You couldn't pay me enough to live here.*

The Strip was sandwiched between the lake and the Skyway Bridge. Seagulls swooped down for morsels of rotting fish and french fries. Angie and I used to take the kids here.

But I clearly remembered the day we'd stopped coming. "Unsafe for Swimming" signs had been posted. Tons of carp had washed up on the beach and were rotting under the hot sun. Swarms of bottleneck flies were everywhere. The stink was putrid. After that, we only took the kids swimming at Turkey Point in July, and the rest of the time to the chlorinated safety of the Irondale Community Center.

"Shut the fuck up, Jerry!" a woman shouted at a barking dog inside the grimy house. I twitched. Dogs didn't usually scare me, but the owner that didn't train a big one right sure as hell did. This dog sounded like a tank.

Nailed above the front door was a sign that looked like a Grade 9 shop class project. "Original Red Demons Motorcycle Club" was unevenly burned into the wood.

The Demons had a long history in Hamilton, and I'd always secretly wondered where their clubhouse was. Now that I knew, I wished I didn't. Bikers made me nervous and angry for a bunch of reasons. Hopefully, this Randy guy wasn't one. But the odds weren't in my favour.

A gleaming Harley Davidson was parked on the weedy lawn. I wasn't impressed. I'd never gotten into hogs like some of my mechanic buddies had. Even as a teen, I'd felt that real men drove cars. Cars with big motors. End of story.

Someone was clomping towards the door. The tank's barking had amped up, and it was scrabbling at the door like it wanted to rip me apart.

"Screw one biker and you screw them all," John liked to say. Yeah, it was a bad idea to mess with these guys, yet here I was at their front door.

Obviously, Randy wasn't a very good mechanic, or maybe he was shit with money, because how else could you explain him living in this shack?

The door swung open.

The woman was gripping a baseball bat and looked like she'd used it before, but not at the diamond. Her hair was the colour of rust, with streaks of grey. Under a huge belt buckle, her belly pooched in her jeans.

I could tell Life had given her more than a few swift kicks to the head and she'd delivered as good as she'd got, in her worn-out cowboy boots.

Beside her, a Doberman was whimpering, vibrating.

"What the fuck are *you* looking at, asshole?" Her t-shirt said, "Swing Low Sweet Chariots". She was braless, and her breasts really were low-swinging. She could easily have tucked them into her belt.

The tips of my ears were burning.

The Doberman was whining louder, eyeing its owner for the signal to rip me apart. It began fixating on my balls, licking its chops.

"You here to try to sell me something, asshole?" Her voice was rougher than the gravel in her driveway. She smacked her palm with the bat. Jerry whimpered even louder.

"Uh, no ma'am. I'm looking for a guy named Randy."

"Randy?" She rolled her eyes and tutted. She tipped her bat towards the tall garage at the end of the driveway.

I was about to thank her but she'd already slammed the door in my face. The dog started barking its head off, lunging at the door again.

I breathed a huge sigh of relief. My balls were safe for another day.

Then, I heard her say, in a gruff voice, "Ready for the *teat*, Jerry?" And the dog began whimpering in a way that made me really uncomfortable.

I prayed to God her husband's name was also Jerry. I hurried down the worn steps.

The garage was basically a tarpaper shack, high enough to store boats or trucks. Smoke curled out of a wonky chimney. One side of the roof sagged. The shingles were puckered and worn.

From inside, I heard muffled music.

My work boots crunched against the gravel as I walked past a black Ford F150. Behind it was a metal sprint car trailer. *Nice.* I knocked on the weathered door.

No answer.

I knocked louder.

"Door's open!" a voice stapled through the music, and the singing resumed.

The guy was the size of a hobbit, sporting a massive porn star moustache. He had a crew cut, and he was wearing what looked to be authentic Nascar coveralls. He was wearing those wrap-around sunglasses opthalmologists give old folks after their cataract surgery. Butt ugly.

He was playing an old upright piano and singing "Georgia". He didn't care in the slightest that a stranger was standing in his garage.

Something about him niggled me, and part of my brain knew why but not the part that formed words.

In the center of the room a golden beast of a sprint car sparkled under fluorescent lights. Black Quaker State and Hoosier decals, America Racer wheels, and a big arse right rear Hoosier tire. It took my breath way.

Past the car hoist, there was a cot, a widescreen tv, bar fridge, and a woodstove in the corner. When I was a teenager, I would have killed for a place like this.

I was beginning to feel pissed that he was ignoring me. The polite thing to do was wait for him to finish. Fuck that.

"Hey! Are you gonna talk to me, pal?"

He slammed his hands against the keys and spun around, his head still bobbling.

Then he stared up at the metal ceiling as if he'd noticed aliens crawling through a hole up there. His sunglasses were channelling Ray Charles. He was serenading an old pink and white Teddy bear sitting on top of the piano. It's sad little face frowned down at him.

Was he blind? Two fries short of a Happy Meal?

"Shh!" he whispered. "Goldilocks is resting." His speech was blunt and rapid-fire.

"Goldilocks?"

Without looking, he pointed at the sprint car.

"Oh, that Goldilocks," I said cautiously. Oh man, Randy was a weird one, alright.

He tossed a Chiclet in the air and expertly caught it in his mouth.

"They told me you were coming," he said, getting to his feet.

"I saw you catch that gum, buddy," I said. "I'm pretty sure you're not blind."

He faced me, grinning.

"Eyesight is over-rated. I choose to *build* blind. Touch trumps sight. Built Goldilocks blindfolded." He made a bizarre coughing sound.

"Sprint Car USA hated my methods. So did the National DIRT Car Association. Blacklisted me. Lifetime ban."

"Wow," I said, stunned by his revelation. He was a genius after all. And fucking crazy.

"Nod's as good as a wink to a blind bat."

"Okaaay," I said under my breath.

His head moved jerkily, as if he was trying to track a pinball in his mind.

Next to this guy, Donny was the poster child for normal. I drew in a deep breath to keep from freaking out.

"So, I'm guessing you're Randy."

He finally removed his dark glasses. There were circular bandages over both eyes. So, the guy wasn't blind? Then why the bandages? Majorly confused, I stared at him.

Then the *penny* dropped. Even with the bandages, I recognized him! "You're Randy Rocket? *The* Randy Rocket? *USA Super Dirt Track* Randy Rocket? Head mechanic for Jack McCreadie! Ricky Unser's number one? The genius who fixed Billy Sheppard's busted engine block in record time and he still got the checkered flag? *And* made him rookie of the friggin' year?"

"Threw my chi into that bitch. And Billy ran 'er hard. Billy understood me. Owners, not so much."

What a trip! Not only was he crazy, Randy Rocket was way smaller than he'd looked on tv, or the way I'd remembered him from two years earlier. Angel and me had spent an entire weekend down at the Oswego Raceway in New York, watching him work his magic in the pit during the Federline Auto Parts Super DIRT Week. He'd been in charge of Dale Sanderson's Big Block modified car, and of course Dale had won.

Despite all that, I still found myself star-struck.

"You're a freakin' legend. What the hell are you doing in Hamilton? And how the hell did you get tangled up with Beppe and Toto?"

"Three divorces. Five kids. Alimony. Guys on my teams couldn't handle my methods. Called me mental. No one would hire me." He double-tapped his nose with his middle finger. "Sucks to be a genius. Lobotomy time."

I felt a stab of empathy for him. He'd obviously lost his mind. And was hiding from his responsibilities in a shitty part of Hamilton, of all places, far from the big-time raceways. Wrenching on Giorgio's car wouldn't pay enough to cover alimony. Unless it was so important to Beppe that he was paying Randy a fortune to make sure Giorgio won? Something didn't add up.

"Beppe made me an offer I couldn't refuse," he said. "Giorgio. Good kid. Innocent. Rare. I follow the work. So here I am."

Bullshit.

"Can you take those bandages off, man? They're freaking me out."

"Absolutely not. That's it, that's all." He defiantly folded his arms over his chest.

"Unbelievable," I muttered.

In a photo on the wall behind him, he had his arm slung over Dale Earnhardt's shoulder. He really was *the* Randy Rocket, although he was now the crazy version, unless he'd always been that way and it had gotten worse.

"You said methods." My brain had finally registered his word from earlier. "What methods?"

"The ones that make drivers win. They can't handle it. Especially Jack McCreadie. But I still got my super suit, so I'm ready when the Nascar boys come crawling back."

I stared at his duds. He was wearing the typical one-piece racing suit, with a few of the kinds of patches you'd expect—Valvoline, Shell, and the stars and stripes. Nothing special here. Great. I was dealing with another Norb. "So, Rocket, is *this* your special suit? Can you fly in it?" Yeah, I know, I was being an a-hole, but I was getting pretty sick and tired of being surrounded by crazy.

Randy scoffed. "Of course not, you think I'm nuts? I'm not going to walk around in my super suit."

To distract myself, I focussed on some photos on the wall. Ricky Unser was receiving his third Nascar trophy, but awkwardly standing beside him was some guy in a shiny...spacesuit?

Beside it, Randy had taped up a schematic. Mathematical calculations surrounded a similar type of suit that made me think of a sci-fi movie robot. Even more bizarre was the braided shielded wire he'd wrapped around an old vintage tv set. One end attached to a steel pipe that stuck out of the concrete floor. I knew enough about car electronics to know the wire was there to ground radio signals. But the number of turns and the thickness was way over the top. What was wrong with this guy?

Randy followed my gaze and barked out a bitter laugh. "Unser was stubborn. Volatile. But he saw me do my thing. Last straw. Went nuts. Punched me in the nose. Fired me. Ratted me out to the organization." He triple-tapped his nose.

"Ricky Unser punched you out?"

"Mmm, traumatic. Zippy ding-dong squanto."

"Zippy ding-dong what?" I clenched my fists. To distract myself again, I decided to take a closer look at Goldilock's engine. I have to say, it was pretty damn sweet.

"Those cylinder heads are beauts."

"And she's got serious torque," Randy said.

I decided to move things along in this bizarre conversation. "So, I guess you know why I'm here."

"The Sicilian, yeah. He told me. You and me. Gonna wrench this beauty. Winner. Chicken dinner." He gave the car a loving kiss.

"Uh, I'm pretty sure Beppe's not Sicilian. Look, I've gotta work with you, but you need to get yourself together, Rocket. OK? If you lose it on this assignment, Giorgio will lose, or get disqualified. Then we're fucked. *I'm* fucked. My *family's* fucked! And I can't have that!"

He squared up with me, face suddenly hostile. "Tony Valentini. Sad-sack family man. Coward. Wasted his talent fixing mediocre cars for mediocre people at mediocre Canadian Tire." His words stapled faster, sharper. "Hamilton nutcase. King of Regret. Your Majesty." And he gave me an elaborate, snarky bow.

I balled up my trembling fists. "Nutcase? Fuck you, Rocket! You should talk!"

I could barely think straight. I fought not to pound him. I was sick knowing I needed this guy so badly.

He stepped into me. "Who made you quit, Prodigy? Huh? The wife? Did she cut off your balls off and shove them in her purse? Or did *you* just gently slide them in there?"

I swung my fist at his head. I didn't frickin' care that his eyes were still bandaged. But with unbelievable awareness, he dodged away, Donny-style, and dove under the car. I got down on my knees and saw him cradling his state-of-the-art Donovan 410 engine block like a love. Tears were leaking through his bandages.

"She wants you to put her hands on her," he said, suddenly gentle. "Do it, Tony! She commands you!"

"Fuck you, Randy!" But something about his engine-love touched me, even though I knew it was totally fucked up.

"Feel her chi, Tony!" he cried, joyously. "It's even more beautiful when she's running."

I was too shocked to respond. I knew that chi was some kind of Chinese energy. Donny had taken chi gung for six months, convinced he'd found the Holy Grail and was going to teach it full-time but then, predictably, had quit.

I felt compelled to play along. Otherwise, Randy might never come out from under the car. I reached under the frame and put my hand on the block. The engine was warm.

"Giorgio *will* win!" he cried.

"Said the blind mechanic." Still, I did appreciate the commitment. We'd need every bit of skill we could gather.

He ripped off a single eye-bandage. "Even a blind pig can find an acorn once in a while!"

He thumbed the bandage back on.

Was I going to have to put up with crap like this for the next seven weeks? "What are you friggin' on about? Blind pig? Acorn? Just talk like a regular person, pal."

He vibrated out from under the car. In one fluid motion, he jumped up and stood ram-rod straight, saluting me. I swallowed down my anger, which was rising again.

Like a mellow maestro, he sauntered over to the piano. He slipped his shades back on and started playing, "Don't Let the Sun Catch You Crying"

I didn't know whether to laugh, cry, or kick him in the head.

Had he set up our entire conversation so he could bang out this tune as some kind of grand finale?

He called out over his music. "Tomorrow. Seven p.m. Hermonville Raceway. Goldilocks. Test-drive."

Something about that time niggled me. Then a lightbulb went off. "Sorry, I can't. I have to take my daughter to swimming lessons." There was no way I was going to let this crazy B.S. interfere with my family life.

"Bus time for the kid!" he sang. "Solo effort! Daddy needs to let go! Kid needs to grow up! *Scoo-bee-doo-wap-de-boo-waaa*!" He paused for a moment, ditched the jazz shit, then hit the Pacemakers tune again.

"You nervy little fucker!"

I'd promised myself I'd never let Angel or my other kids down and so far I hadn't, not like Dad had with Josie and me. But now I suspected that I might not be able to be there for my daughter while also trying to save Ma from financial ruin.

Then Randy started burp-singing and I lost it. "Shut the fuck up, Rocket!"

He didn't miss a beat.

I stormed out of the garage.

Next door, Jerry-the-Doberman was still barking his head off.

If I was lucky, maybe he'd break through the door and eat Randy for dinner.

Chapter 5

THE DELICIOUS AROMA of chicken parmigiana and garlic bread hung in the dining room, where we kept the chandelier light low during Sunday dinner. I figured it would be better to break the bad news after we ate. My wife's amazing cooking always put people in a good mood.

Angie and I had some red wine to polish off before clean-up. Angie was the love of my life, *my* Sophia Loren, if Sophia had a big nose and a bit of a gut. But that's not mean to say, because, to me, Angie was beautiful.

She was more pit bull than movie star, and way smarter than me, and had a heart the size of Italy. Mine was the size of a ball bearing.

I really had no idea what she ever saw in a fat, bull-headed wop like me. By the time I was twenty-one, I'd looked forty, and now my hands were permanently tattooed with car grease.

Angel had finished dinner and was in the living room watching Power Rangers, happily acting out the fight scenes. She was ten going on twelve, and some days fifteen, and that scared me. My adult daughters, Francesca and Viviana, had steady boyfriends and were tree-planting in British Columbia to help pay their university tuition. Frankie lived in Calgary, Alberta, and drove long-haul truck. He'd always hated school. Recently, he'd proposed marriage to his high school sweetheart—chip off the old block!—and now we had a wedding to look forward to. Things were looking up for the Valentini family. Or, they had been, until now.

"What's bugging you, Tone?" she asked, her voice lowered. She sipped some red wine.

"That obvious, huh?"

"Yup."

I leaned forward so I could see through the kitchen into the living room. Thankfully, Angel was totally immersed in battle—she wasn't old enough to hear this.

"I have some bad news, Angie."

Her forehead creased.

I told her everything.

When finished with the news that I couldn't take Angel to her swimming lesson, I broke down crying.

Angie squeezed my hand. Her brown eyes were intense. "Your dad's a piece of work, Tone. If I didn't love him, I think I'd hate him for this. But even so, you need to get this Giorgio guy a win for Ma's sake. You just do whatever it takes, okay? I've got your back."

My anger hit the runway and gained speed.

She recognized my pattern and gently shook my shoulder. "Focus, big guy. Forget about your dad, think *only* of Ma. Promise me you'll do that, okay?" She shook some more. "*Promise,* Tony."

"All his bullshit is gonna ruin this family," I growled. "Now it's affecting my relationship with Angel, *and* Ma, *and* you, the way it's affected me my whole friggin' life."

I slammed my fist against the table, upending my glass. Wine spilled onto the table cloth. "He was and still is a piece of shi—"

I froze when I saw Angel leaning against the door jam. I hadn't noticed her. How long had she been there? How much had she heard?

See what you do, Dad! You wreck people!

She was the spitting image of her mom at her age, tomboyish, too.

"Dad, I can go to swimming lessons on my own. I'm old enough now."

"No, you're not."

She folded her arms over her chest. "Tiara's parents let her take the bus. We can go together. *Pleeze.*"

"Next year," I said.

She gasped. "Dad! I'm in Grade 5! I'm not a kid anymore."

"No more, *piccolo*. Next year. End of story."

She glowered at me.

When it came to raising kids, I was the opposite of my dad. He'd rarely been home after dinner so Josie and me could have been out stealing cars or selling drugs and he'd have had no idea. I was a little overprotective, but at least *I* was a good dad.

"Angelina," Angie said, "I'm going to drive you to your swimming lesson, okay? Afterwards we'll get take-out."

She perked up. "Chinese food?"

"You bet!" Angie laughed.

Angel hugged her mom, and then I gently tugged her over to me.

"Well," I said, grimly, "how much of our conversation did you hear?"

"Everything," she said matter-of-factly. "I'll be your assistant. I know what all the tools are for."

She did.

I opened my mouth to object, but she had her argument ready.

"If Giorgio Santucci doesn't win, Nonna will end up homeless!" She made a boo-boo lip and teared up. "And Nonno, too, although I know you hate him."

I felt bad she thought that. "No, I don't hate him, Angel. It's...complicated."

She gave me her best skeptical face. "I'm not a baby. Why don't you just explain it to me?"

I looked away.

I'd never told her why I'd shut Dad out. I told her I'd give her the full story when she turned eighteen. It drove her crazy when I said that.

"The main thing is, Nonna and Nonno won't end up homeless, Angel," I said. "I'll make sure Giorgio wins. I promise."

Angie squeezed Angel closer.

"I'm scared," Angel said, searching my face for reassurance.

"Don't worry, kiddo," Angie said. "Your Pops will make everything work out. Right, Pops?"

"Right," I said. "Piccola, I'm sorry that piece-of-garbage Doughboy threw sand in your gas tank." My anger shot from zero to a hundred. "If I had it my way, I'd give that prick a Columbian necktie!"

"Tony!" Angie cried, "watch your mouth!" She glared at me.

Just as suddenly, my rage was replaced with shame. I couldn't believe I'd cursed in front of my daughter *and* threatened violence. In the past I'd bit my tongue so hard I was surprised I still had one.

Truth was that by her age I'd known everything about the mob and the horrible things they did to their victims, and in fact had been fascinated by it.

Angel gave me big eyes. "I know what a Columbian necktie is, Dad."

"You *know* what that is?" Angie said, eyeing me suspiciously. "Who told you *that*?"

"Nevio Costa. He even told me about the Chicago overcoat."

I had no idea my ten-year-old daughter knew about this stuff! What else did she know?

Angie shook her head with disgust. "Wait till I talk to Nevio's ma, then we'll just see who's wearing a Chicago overcoat."

"Don't, Ma," Angel gasped. "Please!"

Angie sighed. "Okay, if you promise no more mafia talk."

"Promise!"

"Honey, do you still want to race?" I asked.

"Of *course* I do Dad! I love it! I love the butterflies in my stomach at the starting line, and the way my heart pounds when I pass someone, or when I cross the finish line first. I want to race every day! And I want to win!"

"That's my girl." At her age, I'd felt exactly the same way. "When I'm done with Giorgio, we'll get you back racing again, okay?"

"Okay!"

She hugged me and flew back into the living room in time to sing along with the Power Rangers' end credits music.

I shook my head at Angie, then looked away with disgust.

"I know," she said softly. "Your dad...always your dad."

My old man's ties with a crime family had not only come back to haunt me but had also torn a hole in Angel's innocence. The gas tank thing was a dirty trick. How dare they fuck with my daughter to fuck with me! And how dare they introduce her to the evil in the world.

Worse, much worse, I'd lied to my daughter. I had no real idea if I could get Giorgio a win.

Suddenly, the thought of letting Angel and Ma down was too much to bear. I wanted to upend the table through the window. *Fuck you, Dad!* I was vibrating. Angie was looking at me like I was a rabid dog. I'd sunk to a new depth. I was losing it!

Before I did something truly awful, I charged away from the table, dragged on my shoes, and stormed out of the house into the hot soupy air. I needed to be alone and think my way out of my nightmare.

After an hour of walking aimlessly, I realized it had gotten dark. Just me and the streetlights. Sweat had stuck my t-shirt to my back. My heart was hiss-thumping in my ears. My neck muscles were a pile of knots. Desperate, I did something I didn't want to do.

Chapter 6

DONNY JOINED ME AT our table all grinned up. "Two meetings in a row, Big Dawg. What-up with that?"

I was getting really sick of his stupid, juvenile humour. Recently he'd apologized to us for laughing at other people's expense. Donny was an adrenaline junkie or attention whore or something, but he was working on it. So he said. I had my doubts.

I guess the look on my face sobered him up.

"Everything okay? Seriously, I'm worried about you, Tony."

"No, everything's not okay. I'll tell you when Norb and John get here." I took a huge slug of my frozen lemonade and immediately got brain freeze.

Donny looked puzzled, then blinked it off.

While he yammered on about some conspiracy theory, I chewed over my own thoughts. I hated sharing my problems. A man should keep them to himself or share them with his wife, if they're that bad. Sharing your shit with middle-aged guy friends was for pussies.

Sure, the guys did that with me, and it had been going on for so long I'd gotten used to it. But I sure didn't like the shoe being on the other foot.

Although, if I was being honest, my friends needed me less these days. Even Norb was finally growing up. Most times when he showed up, he'd bring Hans in one of those baby knapsacks you wear on your stomach, then take off early for playgroup or the library or the playground. I'd never seen a more hands-on dad. But sometimes I did miss the old Norb a little bit, the old Norb who needed me more.

In my anxiety, I found myself "ruminating", as Angie called it, on all sorts of bad stuff from the past. There was the time when Frankie was two, skipping around the living room, and he'd slipped and cracked his frickin' jaw on the fireplace. The poor kid had gone into hysterics. Angie and me had run around like chickens with our heads cut off, trying to stem his bleeding with a tea towel while one of us (we think it was Angie but we could never remember) called 911.

Then there was horrible time The Screw's thugs spray-painted a death threat on our garage door and threatened to kill Norb's family if he didn't flush his Invisiblator idea out of his comic book.

And the time we'd gone Incognito at Norb's shop to set up The Screw, getting him to pull a gun on us, so we could get video of it. It all barely worked out.

I remembered when The Screw had pulled a gun on Norb in front of Irondale Lanes. And had tried to murder everyone at the Tartan Club. Fun times.

And then there was Donny's life in shreds from trying to bring Steven back to life. And John's heartbreak over Sophia.

Well, now it was my frickin' turn. For once, I couldn't shit out my dad problems on my own.

My breathing shallowed-out.

Sheena drove up to the main window, dropped John off, then waved to Donny and me and sped away.

John grabbed a coffee and sat with us.

"Hey, Johnny," I said. "How's the wife?" I was trying to be cool, but all I wanted to do was jump up and yank my hair out like a lunatic.

"Great," he said, his smile all pearly-whites. He saluted Donny, who was now his cousin-in-law, thanks to Sheena.

"And the biz?" I asked.

"Classes are packed. All good."

Just then, he choked on a mouthful of coffee.

Norb had barrelled in wearing a ludicrous pair of Lederhosen. He'd been in love with them ever since he'd worn the Yosh Shmenge disguise at our bogus Murder Mystery. He ran up to us, panting, his cheeks popping like red roses, his voice all whistle-y. "Tony, are you okay? Another meeting? What's wrong? How can I help? Are you in trouble? Did the The Screw break out of jail? Did he threaten you? What does he want?" He lowered his voice and looked around nervously. "Do you want me to put on my Avenger suit and kick his ass? Frack! This is all my fault! I should have been there for you!" He finally ran out of steam.

His eyes darted back and forth. He obviously had more he needed to say, but he seemed to have trouble remembering *or* finding the words, but then he did.

"I'm so sorry we didn't rescue you, Tony. We should have confronted your kidnappers in that minivan. Like *real* superheroes. But that skinny gangster guy was so creepy, we just froze, right, guys?"

"And when we finally made it to the window, Donny said the fat man looked like Wayne Newton and that really freaked us out."

"I said that?" Donny said sheepishly, scratching his cheek.

Donny and Norb gave me an apologetic shrug. They were clearly ashamed for not helping me in my hour of need, but I sure as hell understood. I didn't expect my friends to just start a dust-up with the Cosa Nostra. The sight of Toto and Beppe would have paralyzed me, too, if Ma's welfare hadn't been at stake.

"Sorry, Tony," Donny mumbled.

"Ditto," said John.

"What's with the Lederhosen, Norb?" Donny asked, trying not to grin, but totally failing.

Poor Norb was flustered. "Uh, when Tony called a meeting, I was with Morag, and—" He couldn't finish. He blurted: "I was so afraid I'd be late for Tony's meeting I didn't change my clothes and hurried right over." He was heavy-duty blushing.

At first, I didn't know why he was so flustered then it hit me. He'd been making the sweet love to Morag! I threw up my hands. "*Pfff*, too much information, Norb! Make yourself useful and grab us a box of donuts. Now. Please!"

He was relieved to get away from the table.

Donny was laughing his ass off. John grinned.

"Friggin' guy," I said, shaking my head.

The last thing I wanted carbuncled in my brain was the image of Norb in his weird leather shorts, getting it on with Morag. There are some things a friend shouldn't know.

By the time Norb returned with the donuts, John was jerking with silent laughter. Before marrying Sheena, John would have had a field day cutting Norb up for the way he was dressed, but the new and improved John had held back, and I was impressed.

John took a deep breath to calm himself. "OK, spill Tony. What the hell happened yesterday?"

"Yeah," Donny said. "Who was that guy?"

"Uncle Toto. My dad's pal when I was a kid." *Not such a great pal now is he Dad?*

"Like the Wizard of Oz?"

"Naw. It's an Italian thing. Short for Salvatore."

Norb was listening while inhaling donuts. His blousy white shirt and dirndl were covered in sprinkles. I imagined Mrs. Reingruber brushing them off her little boy and gently scolding him for being so messy. I felt sad, knowing Norb would never see her again, or be her little boy. One day, it would be my turn to lose my mother.

John hooked out a donut before Norb could finish them all off. "That *was* your Dad we saw in the back seat of the van, right?"

My friends hadn't seen him for years. That had been the way I liked it.

"Yep." There was bitterness in my voice.

"That Toto guy gave me the creeps," Norb said.

"Definitely," Donny said. "Probably a stone-cold killer."

Then the guys got really quiet. They'd never seen me so grim.

"Beppe Santucci called in Dad's old gambling debt. Four hundred G's. Beppe will only forgive it if I ensure his son Giorgio wins the Sprint Car Nationals, but if I fail, and I *will*, Ma and Dad will have to sell the house to pay it off."

"Shit, that's a huge debt," John said.

"Well, my Dad's a huge arsehole, so there you go."

"Where will they go if they lose the house?" Norb asked.

"Ma can stay at my house, but my father can go live in a damn sewer, for all I care."

"You could try to forg—" Norb stopped himself. He was going to say *forgive*, but he'd momentarily forgotten just who he was talking to. I wouldn't forgive. We all knew that.

"Maybe your Ma could live in an apartment," Norb offered softly. "My aunt Elkie lived in one her whole life and she was super happy. She lived to be a hundred."

"You're missing the point, Norb," I said, gruffly.

Norb had *thoughts*. "So, Beppe was the guy riding shotgun? The guy who we thought was Wayne Newton? And Doughboy was the driver, right?"

"Yep."

"The driver reminded me of the Pillsbury Doughboy," Donny said.

I'd also described Beppe and Doughboy that way to myself. Somehow being friends living in the Village had wired our brains to describe people the same way.

"His real name is Elio. And I don't know how he's connected. For all I know, he's Toto's son." Just one big, happy family, that crew.

"*Eeelio*?" Donny said. "That's a horrible name. Slimy."

"So, just how evil are these mobsters?" Norb asked. "More evil than The Screw?"

"Hard to say. Toto was packing heat, so there's that."

"Shit," John muttered. "What do these a-holes call themselves?"

"No idea." I paused. "Old Italian Bastards?"

We all laughed weakly.

"Oh, I know! The Cosa Knob-stra," Donny said.

"Oh, oh! The Wizards of Odds!" Norb added. "No, actually, that's kinda cool-sounding."

For once, I didn't roll my eyes when these guys said something stupid. They'd sacked up to help me. Tricky emotions burned in my guts. I realized how much I'd *always* needed Donny and my friends, even if it was just hanging out with them, or playing road hockey, or being their dad figure.

But there was something wrong with this picture. It was like the Lone Ranger begging the Three Stooges for help. The *Lone* Ranger worked alone. That was his whole deal. That was usually *my* deal.

"What can we do?" John asked.

"Yeah," said Norb. "How, Tony, please tell us?"

"I dunno. All I know is tomorrow night I'm going to Hermonville Raceway to meet up with Giorgio and his mechanic, Randy Rocket. Giorgio's gotta win, somehow."

"Randy Rocket?" Donny said, laughing. "Sounds like a porn star."

This time I did roll my eyes, but he was right. "Shit, it does, doesn't it?" Great.

"I don't want to think about porn," Norb said. "I just want to think about Morag."

"You know why you do, Norb? John asked.

"No. Why?" Understandably, Norb looked nervous. After all, it was John talking.

"Because you're a gentleman."

Norb breathed a sigh of relief. "Thanks, John. I appreciate that."

"You're welcome."

I was impressed with John. He really was trying to be a better man. He'd spent decades making Norb the butt of his jokes and jabs.

"So, this Randy guy's a pretty good mechanic?" John asked, tapping his thighs. "Maybe you've got a chance?"

"An *amazing* mechanic," I said. "He's worked on cars at all the big tracks." I didn't mention he was certifiable. "And he always gets Giorgio's car into second place, but Giorgio can't seal the deal. So

Beppe wants me to magically make that happen." I shook my head in disgust. "As if."

Like most people, my friends had no clue about my work as a mechanic or race car driving, just like I had no clue about comic books or salsa dancing or self-published books or editing YouTube videos, and I didn't have the energy to explain to them how crazy Randy was. And I was now seeing first-hand how exhausting it was talking about your problems. I swear I needed to lie down. Maybe this was a mistake.

I was about to leave when Donny whispered in my ear. "I know a guy at the track who can fix a win for your guy."

I flinched. "No!"

"Seriously, for a reasonable price, my guy can rig the race. Think of your Ma, Tony."

"No and no!" Just because I was being strong-armed into helping Beppe didn't mean I was going to break the law to do it.

I got up and headed for the door. But Donny, as usual, was relentless. He tracked in behind me, with his hands cupped around his mouth. "Ten grand, and even the best racer will gladly throw a race."

"Yeah? And what's your cut? Twenty-percent?"

Donny stopped, indignant. He threw his hands on his hips. "What? I don't think so Valentini. Try zero percent. Huh! What kind of friend do you think I am, anyway?"

"Forget it, Donny. And you gotta stop hanging out with crooks. I hate *all* gangsters and *guys*. I'm not gonna cross that line. End of story!"

"Hermonville Raceway is a gambling den. Everything and anything can be bet on. People throw races all the flippin' time!"

I spun around. "How do you know that?"

"I have a crime-writing colleague who covers the crime beat."

"Yeah, well whipty-do. I'm not interested!"

I threw the door closed, but that didn't make me feel any better. I wanted to hold onto something familiar—my wife, my family, a wrench, a carburetor, an Alice Cooper record—anything!

But I knew those fallbacks wouldn't be enough, not anymore. I'd never felt so alone and afraid. Bless my friends, but they sure as hell couldn't help me. "Fuck!"

I got into my truck and cranked the stereo. Alice Cooper's, "You Drive Me Nervous" roared me out of the parking lot onto Flux Road. I was determined to deal with my shit, *alone*, without the help of Donny's sleazeball guy, and I'd do it with the same kick-ass courage as all my friends had shown in the past couple of years: Donny in his "if you build it they will come" moment, Norb when he faced off with that deadly little scumbag, and John when he'd finally hooped all his pride and let Dr. Hotz re-jig his noggin'.

My friends were the lucky ones. They'd gotten over *their* worst. I felt like the last guy waiting in line to jump off a cliff.

And I was so scared and messed up, I ran a red light.

Chapter 7

The Hermonville Raceway felt the same, but *I* was not the same guy who'd once absolutely believed his future was on a podium accepting the cup. Feeling like a total imposter, I parked Angela's old Dodge Caravan in the mostly deserted parking lot. It figures that my truck had decided to spring an oil leak that morning. There'd been no time to fix it.

I walked past five black trucks, and a beautiful 1979 baby blue Ford F-150. I had a thing for old trucks. When I retired, I was going to treat myself to a vintage beater and fix it up.

I'd worn my old red racing suit, hoping it would make me look like I belonged. A lifetime ago, along with my old racing trophies, I'd mothballed it inside the storage trunk behind the furnace. It was wrinkled like an accordion and so tight I was worried it would split and birth the giant meatball that was my gut. It was stupid to wear it. I should have just thrown on my coveralls, but my insecurities were doing a number on my decision-making today.

I nervously tugged at my belt. Angie was right when she said I was an emotional eater. In the past decade, I'd really packed on the beef. Maybe after this was all over, I'd finally go on a diet.

My heart thumped and my adrenaline pumped, the way they used to before a big race. I felt like a giant magnet was pulling me closer. I'd forgotten that feeling, and how much I loved it.

But coming here isn't about you, I reminded myself, *it's about Giorgio. See what makes him tick and fix his shit. Take Goldilocks apart. Put her back together. Take pictures. Study them. Make Dad proud! Dad?* That last thought made me cringe.

I wasn't built for self-analysis, not like John was. My winning strategy had always been to focus harder on my work, to block Dad out of my mind.

The sight of the cinder-block clubhouse made me uneasy. All these years later, it reminded me of a countryside abattoir. And it looked way smaller than I remembered it, almost Bush League. *Shit, I used to think this place was elite.*

Above the entrance, in bold red-lettering, a sign welcomed me to Hermonville Raceway, "Southern Ontario's Premiere Track". A miniature sprint car replica jutted out of the wall, beside a massive Canadian Flag.

Reluctantly, I went through the battered steel doors.

I turned in slow circles, taking it all in.

Framed photos of local track legends lined the walls. I remembered them well. The guys in these photos had been my heroes. The snack bar, washrooms, the trophy case, and the souvenir shop that sold t-shirts, jackets, coffee mugs, and memorabilia, all looked mostly unchanged.

I was about to head out to the track when something caught my eye. Heat filled my gut.

It was a photo of me at twenty, grinning like a shithouse monkey with my trophy, flanked by Larry "Hoffy" Hoffman and Luke Ranger, my old racing pals. We'd had a monopoly on mini-stock wins for a while there. I couldn't believe how young we looked!

Hoffy owned the car, and Luke had been our wizard mechanic, and of course I'd been the driver, the "Prodigy". My heartstrings twanged. I felt the way you do when you're all alone in your car driving and the radio plays that Beatles song, "In my Life," and you get all sentimental for the good old days and you want to start bawlin', like when I was a kid and my cousins had to go back to Italy after summer vacation at our house.

Man, I hadn't let myself think about Luke and Hoffy for years. They'd been like brothers to me. I panged for us and what we'd accomplished. We'd been a special crew, the three of us. I felt shitty for cutting them out of my life.

I sighed a lifetime's worth. I owed my old team mates a serious apology—they'd tried to keep in touch, but I'd shut them down. When I left racing, it was just too painful to think about any of it.

Numbly, I headed out and followed a dirt path between the bleachers and found myself on the track apron for the first time in twenty years.

My skin was tingling. I stared at the sky, trying to block out all the feelings.

The sky was deep blue, the sun low in the sky. A small breeze failed to relieve the humidity. The sodium arc lights hadn't come on yet.

Thankfully, there was no sign of the Three Devils. Maybe they'd stay away and let me work in peace.

I should have been home with Angie enjoying our typical after-dinner walk along the mountain brow, taking in the city scape below the escarpment. Instead, I was stuck in the past, trying to ensure some wop hot-shot won a race he had no right winning because he wasn't good enough.

Crap. I was no better than Donny, trying to make Steven famous. And I was gonna fail. But then I reminded myself that Donny had kind of succeeded for a while. So maybe I could do the same with Giorgio.

I heard the roar of our sprint car. Giorgio was driving Goldilocks, tearing up the far straightaway. A trail of dust hung in the air behind him. He hit the turn a little too tight, but a quick ramp and throttle adjustment and the rear tire grabbed and sailed him seamlessly around the corner. *Nicely done*, I thought. *Maybe I can help you win, after all.*

Up the track apron on my right, an ATV waited to push-start a blue and white sprint car. Drivers shared track times to cut down on rental costs. Even back in my day, the fees had been expensive.

In a nearby pit, two mechanics were shooting the breeze, watching and waiting for Giorgio to swing by, so their guy could fire up and hit the track for his turn.

Two safety crew guys in orange fire suits leaned against a pick-up truck piled high with safety gear, fire extinguishers, and stretchers. Their presence was mandatory, and maybe that was the main reason rentals were expensive, but it was worth it. You didn't want to race without those guys. They might save your life.

Then, along came the legendary Randy Rocket, strutting like a cocky rockstar.

Weirdly, I got shivers, but they turned to shudders the closer Rocket got—he was marching toward me like the T-1000. Frick, the guy was just majorly strange.

Now Randy wasn't alone. Someone had joined him.

The closer they got, the more I was struck by just how small Randy was, maybe even under five feet. Small man, big talent. Like Dustin Hoffman.

Genius or not, I felt bad for the guy. How humiliating and degrading to be kicked out of the majors and forced to work the "C" circuit in Hermonville, Ontario, of all places. And how did he even find out about Hermonville? No one in the big leagues would have a clue about that hick town. It all sounded so fucked up and unlikely. Something was definitely off about the whole thing.

The man with Randy had on a white golf shirt with the track logo. I put him at almost seventy. His skin was darkly tanned and his eyes were hard. Something about him made me uneasy. Maybe he was a decent guy, but maybe he wasn't.

"Joe Messina, track manager. Pleasure to meet you again, Tony."

Reluctantly, I shook his hand, trying to place his face.

Randy pointed at Joe. "My go-to guy."

Joe smiled wider, unfazed by the eye-bandaged, sunglasses-wearing nutbar beside him.

I could tell he knew I didn't recognize him.

"I worked here when they called you the Prodigy," he said. "You were a local hero."

I shrugged. Maybe it was rude, but I felt like he was poking my wound.

"Seven wins in one year," he said, shaking his head in amazement. "An unbroken track record. So impressive. Your future was so bright."

Ouch.

"Why *did* you quit?"

OK. Maybe he didn't know he was being a prick, but I stared him a hard one. "There's more to life than racing cars, Joe." I tried to keep my voice calm and pleasant, but it was tough. "So instead, I raised a family and won at that. Off track, I *am* a hero. And I only came back to help Giorgio Santucci, and then I'm gone. End of story."

It dawned on me why I couldn't remember him. I'd been too cocky and self-centered to remember anyone except for the drivers I had to beat.

Shit, what if Giorgio was an egomaniac, too? The thought of meeting a younger version of myself sickened me.

I found myself thinking about Beppe. There was no way he wasn't involved in *something* illegal here. It had to be gambling. How big was his operation? Province-wide? Was his Windstar a gambling call-center-on-wheels? Did he *own* the people working here? Like Joe Messina? I sure as hell felt like he owned me.

Given what a gambling addict my father was, I wasn't a betting man, so I had no idea if they wagered on laps, times, or wins, or all three.

I remembered reading the series in The Gazette on the Malatesta Family's involvement in the local crime scene, likely written by Donny's friend. But there had been no mention of Beppe. Maybe the reporter had been threatened with a long walk off a short pier.

But if Beppe was a crime boss, then why not just extort drivers to throw the race? Break some knee-caps or something? Why bother with me?

And what exactly had Dad done to pile up such a huge shitload of debt? Even after all his years of gambling, it seemed like a crazy amount.

And why had Beppe forgiven his debt for twenty-five years? Did mobsters ever do that?

A sprint car flew off the track and skidded in beside us, kicking up a dust screen.

Giorgio waved at me through the clearing dust. I wondered what it would be like to be behind the wheel of that gorgeous golden sprint car. I was so envious.

He sprang out and skipped over to me with his helmet tucked under his arm. Maybe thirty years old, he was easily six foot five, with olive skin and a crew cut. In his form-fitting green and white racing suit, with his muscled physique, he could have passed for a male model or a CFL quarterback or a good-looking farm hand.

He tore off a glove and shook my hand. His grip was powerful. *Blue-eyed Italian*, I thought, absent-mindedly. *Northern Italy*. A rare sighting, like suddenly spotting a grizzly bear rambling down Flux Road. He must have gotten his looks from his Ma, because he didn't look anything like dad, Wayne Newton, thankfully. He was so tall he made Randy look like a garden gnome. I wondered how he managed to squeeze into the sprint car.

"The Prodigy!" he cried. "It's such an honour to finally meet you!" He grinned, star-struck. Oh, I sure hoped he wasn't another weirdo.

"I'm no Prodigy," I said. "Middle-aged burn-out, more like it. I haven't driven a rig in twenty years."

Randy's head was bobbling. What the hell was going on in that crazy noggin?

Suddenly, I was losing my temper—again. "That asshole Doughboy dumped sand in my daughter's gas tank. She's just ten! Did you know about that, Giorgio?"

He gasped and clamped his hands against his cheeks. It was like watching the *Home Alone* kid.

"That's terrible!" he said, his brow crinkled. "Who would do such an awful thing? Especially to an innocent kid. I'm so, so sorry, Tony. I promise you, I'd never be part of that! Please, who is this Doughboy?"

Maybe he was innocent. "One of your Papa's dickhead cronies. Drives a Ford Windstar? Looks like an evil Pillsbury dough boy?"

"Oh, dear, dear," he tutted. "That was my step brother, Elio. Elio's *not* a nice person. He used to bully me."

I bet that skeezy Elio didn't mess with this big boy now.

Giorgio continued. "If he did put sand in your daughter's gas tank then I'm so sorry he did, but I honestly don't know anything about that. And I kind of don't want to know." He shook his head sadly. "My papa's business is a secret, and that's the way I like it."

Shit. He was cuckoo for Cocoa Puffs. Just like friggin' Randy. I was screwed!

"I'm sure Pappa had nothing to do with that," Giorgio said, "He's a good person. But I'm sorry your daughter didn't win the race. That must have been really hard on her, and you, of course."

I relaxed, a little. This guy had a mobster father, but Giorgio seemed innocent. Hell, we can't be held responsible for the sins of our fathers, right?

"Shoot!" he cried, exuberantly. "Almost forgot. My main man!"

He blew past me and began fist-bumping Randy. Like a couple of dopey twelve-year-olds, they elbow-bumped, twirled, over-underred, hand-slapped, foot-dragged, then sang, "Hit the Road Jack", a song made famous by Ray Charles. A final fist bump and Randy jockeyed past me and popped open the hood.

I couldn't believe how depressed I was having to work with these oddballs. If it wasn't for Ma, I swear I would have killed myself.

Giorgio waved me over.

I was pretty sure that whatever Randy was doing with the engine would piss me off or freak me out.

Was he trying to cast a spell on it? Trying to have sex with it? It was probably better not to know!

Man, I'd never felt so pressured, weirded out, and helpless. Next to these two yahoos, Donny Love was the patron saint of normal.

As we headed for the car, Giorgio said, "I still feel really sorry for Tommy. It wasn't his fault I didn't win. But Papa was so upset, he fired him." He laughed good-naturedly. "Papa and his temper! Oh boy."

I really didn't want to think about Papa Beppe's temper. "Who's Tommy?"

"My former mechanic, Tommy Fairview. He was the best. But Papa blamed Tommy." He sounded regretful. "It really was my fault."

I figured I didn't know the real story. "Can I ask you a question, Giorgio?"

"Sure thing! Anything for you, Prodigy!"

"Do you want to win? I mean *really* want to win."

"Heck, yeah!"

It was like talking to the Beav. I was pretty sure Beppe had home-schooled Giorgio and raised him in a bomb shelter. But it was time for this naïve man-child to grow up a little.

I grabbed his arm. "Listen, Giorgio. Do you know why I'm really here?"

"To help me win," he said, uncertainly.

You really don't know, do you? "Yeah, but why did your dad bring *me* in, specifically?"

"Because you have monster skills and talent?"

"Maybe. But the main reason I'm here is because *your* Dad called in the chips on *my* dad's gambling debt, and if you don't win, he's on the hook for 400 grand. My parents would have to sell their house, and that would only pay off half the debt. Ma loves her house. It will kill her to lose it. And they're too old to go back to work, so they'll basically be stuck in a crummy apartment eating dog food. Now, I would never let that happen, so that's how your loving father is twisting my arm. By playing on my love for my mother. Nice, huh?"

Giorgio's mouth was hanging open. "My papa did *that*? Are you sure? I mean, I guess he's not perfect, but...gosh, are you sure you didn't misinterpret everything? I mean, that's just so mean."

I shook my head. This kid just couldn't see the truth about dear old dad. "Giorgio, I can tweak you a better car, I can give you amazing driving advice—hell, I won seven races in a single season— but I can't *make* you win. Only *you* can do that. Capeesh?" I sighed. "Giorgio, why do *you* think you *can't* win?"

I did feel bad for Giorgio. I remembered how anxious I'd felt before a race, but for me it went away once the flag dropped. And how much more anxious must he feel, knowing my parents would lose their house if he didn't win? Unless he didn't give a shit and was secretly playing along for some other reason.

"Oh, that's easy. In the last lap of every race, I get super anxious, especially on the turns. It's like I'm floating out of my body. And I always slide back to second place, even when I'm way ahead." His cheeks went red. "That's why people call me the Second Place Slider."

"I'm sorry, Giorgio," I said. "That's some serious shit you're dealing with." *If it's not made up that is.*

He chewed at his lip.

There was a river of sweat pouring down my brow. The stress and the humidity were getting to me. Giorgio watched me mop my forehead, and then he was suddenly beaming at me.

"'Do not grieve, for the joy of the Lord is your strength.'"

He was quoting the Bible?

"That's from Nehemiah," he added cheerfully. "Lots of great advice in the Bible, you know. Best book ever!" He switched gears. "Tony, listen, I want to win for your parents. And you're a good son, doing this for them. A *great* son."

"You don't know that."

"And your dad was right when he told me how important family is to you."

I tensed up. "He told you that?"

"Yes-siree."

I wasn't surprised he'd spoken to Dad—the track had always been a small incestuous world full of gossip. But who the hell was Dad to pretend he respected our family after he'd done everything in his power to destroy it?

Giorgio spoke softly. "Like your dad, mine is far from perfect, but he loves me dearly and I love him. John 16:33: "In this world you will have trouble. But take heart! I have overcome the world." He smiled like a cherub. "So, what do you say, Tony? Wanna help me overcome the world *and* win the finals?"

Although I still regularly went to Mass, all this Bible talk made me uncomfortable. Then I saw Randy gently kissing the butterfly valves, and the bizarreness of the moment was complete.

I realized the crazy here was totally unfixable, so I decided I'd just have to go with it, for now. "Sure! Why not! Let's do it!"

Giorgio clapped me on the back. He had a strong arm. "I knew you'd be a believer, Tony! I just knew it! That's so awesome!"

It was hard not to like Giorgio. I'd never met a sweeter guy.

We fell in with Randy.

Learn everything you can, I told myself. *He may be certifiable, but he's a genius.* I had my digital camera with me so I could take pictures and study them later.

"Hey, Randy," I said, forcing myself to be cool. "Do you mind if I drop into your garage after work and hang with Goldilocks?"

Randy caressed the valves. "Door's open. Prodigy let's himself in. Zippy ding-dong."

"Great." *Zippy ding-dong, my ass.*

The blue and white sprint car I'd seen earlier skidded in behind us. I'd been too busy to notice it tearing around the track. The hot summer sun had baked the dirt. The dust was choking.

"Tanner!" Giorgio cried.

The driver jumped out and they hugged. Tanner reminded me of a taller, tanned version of Toronto Maple Leafs hockey great Dougie Gilmour. Like Giorgio, he looked to be all apple-pie.

"Tanner Hunt," Giorgio said, "I'd like you to meet our new mechanic and former raceway champ, Tony Valentini, aka the Prodigy."

"The Prodigy!" He went limp. "Oh my God, so awesome to meet you, sir!" He pumped my hand.

How could a corrupt asshole like Beppe have produced such a nice kid? Something didn't add up.

"Nice to meet you, too," I said to Tanner. All this pleasantness was hard work for a leather-heart like me. And yeah, it's nice to be admired, but it was getting to be a bit much, now.

"Tanner and I grew up together," Giorgio offered. "After school, we raced dirt bikes in the back forty behind my barn."

I just nodded. I was ready for social hour to end. It was time to get to work on the car.

"Great day for a spin!" Tanner cried. He jogged to his car and tore off onto the track, out of sight.

"Hey, Tony," Giorgio chirped, "you should take Goldilocks for a spin! She's waiting for you!"

The pang I got at that idea threw me, but I resisted. "Naw, you first, so I can study the way she moves."

"Drive that bitch!" Randy roared. "Love 'er! Feel 'er! Talk to 'er!"

He was crouching down beside the car like a deranged monkey.

To be honest, Goldilocks was hypnotizing me, the way my mini-stock car once had. I felt powerless against it.

"Randy's right," Giorgio said, anxiously. "You need to get a feel for how she handles so you can make her the best she can be." He steepled his hands. "Please, Tony."

"Okay, okay, take it easy. I'll drive it. Relax."

Giorgio looked like a kid who'd just discovered a freezer full of popsicles.

I looked around suspiciously. Maybe Beppe and his goons were watching me, to see if I'd come through.

But the stands were empty, and the safety guys and Tanner's pit crew were busy yakking.

How could I resist?

For two decades, I was terrified that if I ever stepped into a racing car again, I'd get addicted again. Then I'd end up being an absent father, like Dad. By the grace of God, I'd somehow kept that particular needle out of my arm. But now, all these years later, my damn dad was sticking it back in! Shit!

Giorgio handed me his helmet. "Have you driven a sprint car before? I know you used to drive a mini stock."

"No. But I'll figure it out."

"Confident," said Giorgio. "I like that."

Randy was standing with his hands in his back pockets, humming "Bad, Bad Leroy Brown," head tilted up at the sky. He was still wearing those damn eye bandages. Guess the mother ship was just going to signal him through the chip in his neck.

Trying to hide my nerves, I climbed inside the car and squeezed Giorgio's helmet onto my head. It pinched my temples. "This is way too tight."

Giorgio whipped over to our pit stop and returned with two more helmets. One of them fit well enough.

He and Randy backed away a step. Randy headed off to get the push-truck.

I strapped myself into the car.

I found the ramp lever. I knew how it worked from reading Hot Rod magazine and watching YouTube videos. Also, once you've driven a micro sprint and re-built a vintage Camaro *and* wrenched on every kind of car there is for a living, you get a feel for things.

"The valve lever keeps you tight or loose on the turns," Giorgio said, happily leaning in through the window.

"Thanks, Einstein," I snapped, feeling defensive. Well, well. My racing ego had re-surfaced. Maybe it was just what I needed to pull this off.

"After a few laps, you'll get the hang of it. First you click the gear—"

"I know how a sprint car starts, Giorgio, I'm the fucking Prodigy, remember?" I was back to being my younger shithead self. Not good. I took a very deep breath. "Sorry, Giorgio, I'm totally stressed out."

"Of course you are, totally understandable." He was all smiles. "But don't worry, you'll be great." He gave the hood a hearty slap and backed away.

Randy drove up in a black pick-up and snugged the front of it against my bumper, ready to push-start me.

I clicked the gear shift into place, opened the fuel tap, and gave Randy a thumbs-up. He began pushing.

Before I knew it, the oil gauge struck fifty. I hit the start switch. Then I feathered the throttle and the car fired off. I'd hit the gas pedal too hard, discovering it was hot. I was thrown back into my seat! I was off and running! Holy shit!

The adrenaline rush was unbelievable and familiar. I whooped with joy.

All at once, I was struck with how much I'd missed racing, how much it had meant to me, how fricking happy it had made me, and how I'd been so great at it, and how I'd thrown it all away because I couldn't forgive my old man. For the first time since I'd quit, I admitted to myself I should have stuck with racing, that it wasn't all Dad's fault.

Tears stung my eyes and rolled down my cheeks. I shook myself. You can't drive and cry, not with a sprint car going two hundred kilometers per hour.

I throttled hard. Goldilocks was powerful. I swear, I felt like that car was made for me. I reached up and grabbed the valve and pulled the wing back. The car over-tightened so I ran loose, then tight, semi-loose, semi-tight, controlling the swing of my rear tire through the first turn. By the second lap, I felt pretty confident.

After five wild, life-affirming laps, I skidded into the pit stop. Jacked with adrenaline, I practically leapt out of the car. Giorgio and Randy tore up to me. Giorgio's eyes were wide.

"Unbelievable!" Giorgio said, thumping me on the back. "First time out and you slid through the corners like a champ! No wonder they called you the Prodigy."

"*Tight*," Randy offered, jutting out his chin. He pointed at Goldilocks. "Engine. Pronto."

He zipped around me and popped the hood. The block was pretty damn hot, but while we waited for it to cool, Giorgio and me listened to Randy comment on the specs and performance.

"The car was greased lightning," I said. The car's performance had been stellar. "Nice job, Rocket."

"Isn't she a *beaut*?" Giorgio said.

Randy acted like he hadn't heard me. He was now busy studying the engine.

To make sure he really was the same Nascar genius he'd once been, and that insanity hadn't gradually robbed him of his intellect, I challenged him with technical questions about the engine.

His answers were spot on, but when his explanations started to include physics and complex math involved, I zoned out. That stuff was way beyond me.

Giorgio was spellbound. He was *too* fascinated with Randy's explanation, and if anyone else had been there with me, they would have thought the same thing.

"Giorgio, are you okay?"

"Holy cow!" he cried, startled. He palmed his heart. "You scared me."

"Giorgio," I said. "Rocket built you a helluva ride. And we know Goldilocks is obviously not the problem." I paused. "So what exactly makes you so anxious in the final lap? Are you *afraid* to win?"

He stared up past the chain link fence to the bleachers and his expression changed. Half-way up were Toto and Beppe. They smiled and waved to me like phoney-baloneys.

Giorgio pried his gaze away from his dad. "I'm not afraid to win, Tony. I want that more than anything. But like I said, I panic on the final turns. Maybe it's the drifting that makes me anxious." He gulped. "Or maybe I'm so terrified of disappointing Papa. He really wants me to win."

He turned and kicked the tire. It was the first negative emotion I'd seen the kid exhibit. "I'm the Second Place Slider, darn it! I'm cursed! I'll never win! Never!" Suddenly, Giorgio was a tall slice of *sour* apple pie.

Randy made a weird flick of his hand. "No winner, no chicken dinner. Giorgio, you can do this. The Prodigy will help you. Your old man will be happy. Me, too. Bookies, too. Three birds, one stone!"

I fought to understand his crazy talk. Was Randy betting on Giorgio? And what about Beppe? Was he really so desperate for Giorgio to win that he would ruin my Ma and Dad in the process?

Randy had gone full-on bobblehead, swaying and twitching.

I couldn't believe he was the same mechanic I'd idolized since my teens. "What the fuck's wrong with you, Rocket?" I cried.

He launched into singing Ray Charles' tune, "Get On The Right Track, Baby." The music pulled Giorgio out of his temper tantrum. He threw his arm over Randy's shoulder and joined in. It was like watching Talent Night at an insane asylum, but I have to admit—they were pretty good.

"Cut the bullshit!" I cried. "We have a race to win!"

But they were determined to finish.

Now, I have developed a bit of tolerance for nutty people. After all, Donny Love and Norbert Reingruber are my friends. Need I say more? But this? Full-on madness. It was like witnessing major LSD fuckery.

At first, I'd thought that I had half a chance of helping Giorgio. But now that I knew he was as crazy as Randy, I had serious doubts.

Just because they hadn't demonstrated enough craziness, when they finished singing, they launched back into their insane fist-bumping routine. *My* anxiety ran up a pole.

If I didn't get away from them, I'd kill them. I stomped down the track, clenching my fists and yelling some pretty rude words.

They'd done it! They'd made *me* crazy!

It took me about ten minutes to calm down enough to look back, hoping they'd gotten control of themselves so we could get down to work.

But they hadn't! They were still acting bananas. Their faces were full of freakin' joy!

I sank into black depression—the race was over before it had begun.

Even if I helped Randy Rocket work *magic* on the car, if Giorgio hadn't won by now, he was never going to win. He just didn't have the right stuff. Never had. End of story!

Still, as hopeless as the situation was, I knew I had to keep trying. Because I was a good son.

Finally, the kooks bent over, catching their breath, laughing like maniacs. Randy cupped his hands around his mouth and howled like a wolf.

Of course, Giorgio nodded in agreement.

My neck ached with a painful knot. I tried unsuccessfully to knead it out.

My hands were shaking. Probably my blood pressure was through the roof. Angie would be just *thrilled* about that.

Like a shot, the craziness, the heat, the stress, and the pressure to win rag-dolled me against the chain-link fence. I sank down on my butt.

I felt bad for swearing at some poor mentally ill nut. Shit, I needed Randy *and* Giorgio. What kind of leader was I, freaking out in front of the troops like that? I should be firing them up to win. There was too much riding on this for me to lose it like that. I got to my feet and trudged over to them.

"Look, I'm sorry, guys," I said, shaking my head. "I think the heat got to me or something. Sorry for being such an asshole."

Giorgio clapped me on the back and gave me a big smile. Randy gave me some kind of weird hand gesture. It reminded me of Father Theo giving the blessing.

I felt walloped by dread. How exactly was I going to achieve Beppe's demands?

I thought about Norb, who'd faced a truly terrifying, life-or-death scenario. Despite *his* fear, Norb had fought like a goddamn hero. And if he could, I would—somehow.

That's what my life had come to, I thought. *Norbie* Reingruber is now my role model. Shit.

Chapter 8

GIORGIO AND I WERE watching Randy tear out of the darkened parking lot in his truck. When I'd realized that the guy was getting behind the wheel with his eyes still bandaged, I'd freaked.

Giorgio had grabbed my arm. "Wait!" he'd said softly. "He'll take them off, don't worry! He always does it this way. Just give him privacy."

As we watched, Randy nervously glanced around, then carefully pulled off the bandages. Then the nutbar put on his sunglasses and hit the gas, like frickin' Corey Hart.

I consoled myself knowing that, if ever a guy could drive a car home at night in shades, without killing himself or somebody else, it was Randy Rocket. "Why the hell does he do that?" I muttered, more to myself than the kid.

Giorgio tilted his head, "I think he's afraid for people to see his eyes."

John had once told me to accept Donny as he was, not try to change him. He was right, I eventually realized, but I wasn't sure I could do that with Randy.

I leaned against my van and scrubbed a hand down my face. Crickets were making a racket in the surrounding woods.

"Giorgio, I think you should see a psychologist to help you overcome your anxiety."

Giorgio uneasily shoved his hands into the back pockets of his jeans. He was wearing a pair of well-worn cowboy boots and a cowboy hat. He looked like a regular cowpoke. "A psychologist?" Just saying the word made him nervous, you could tell.

"Yeah, a psychologist," I continued. "Look, I get it, but honestly, it's nothing to be scared about, Giorgio. Dr. Hotz did wonders for my buddy, John, and *he* was a total mess."

Giorgio looked doubtful. "So, what was your friend's problem?"

"His wife walked out on him. One day he wakes up and she's gone. Just moved out. No explanation. He took it really hard, like every day for seventeen years. First love and all. She really fucked him up." I left out the part about John's suicide attempt. It was too painful to talk about.

I could see pity in Giorgio's eyes. "I guess first love break-ups can be really hard," he said.

I raised my eyebrow at him. "You never had a break-up?"

He shook his head. "I've always wanted a girlfriend, I just haven't had any luck that way." *Of course, you haven't, you poor, gullable dope. Beppe probably gelded you so you can only focus on winning him a shitload of dough.*

"Just go see Dr. Hotz," I said.

Giorgio frowned. "I don't think Papa would go for me seeing a psychologist. He says all the answers to man's problems can be found in the Bible."

My patience was wearing thin. "Look, I'm Catholic, so I get the whole Bible thing, right? But sometimes people need modern treatments and stuff. Anyway, go see Alice Hotz."

"Do you really think she can cure my anxiety?"

"We all better hope so."

"Okay, I'll see her. Promise. I want to make everyone happy. Especially Papa."

"Good. Her number's in the yellow pages."

"Thanks, Prodigy!"

Giorgio's desperation to please his dad stirred up my own Daddy issues. But I bucked against them before they took hold. "Look, kid, just call me Tony. No more Prodigy shit, alright?"

I had no doubt Beppe had put a lot of money on the upcoming race, and from what Randy had said, others had too.

I still wondered if he would honour his word and forgive Dad's massive debt if Giorgio won. And how could such a sweet kid love such a scumbag of a father?

But whatever the eventual outcome, I was sure Beppe wouldn't lose his son's love. Giorgio seemed incapable of holding a grudge. I could tell he had a heart of gold. Easily as big as Norb's. Maybe even bigger. And not small like mine.

"Tony," Giorgio said.

"Yeah?"

"I was really hoping you were going to give me some pointers."

"Pointers? What for? I saw you drive. You're easily as good as I ever was, maybe better. And you nailed the turns."

"But I wasn't in a real race."

"Don't worry about that. Fix your anxiety and you'll win the Nationals. Guaranteed."

"Really?" He kicked the dirt. "I dunno." He paused, hesitating. "Sometimes I wonder if Papa wants me to race because of money, not because it makes me happy."

Well, well. Maybe the kid had a few more smarts than I'd given him credit for. "Why do you think that? I mean, if that's true, that's pretty low." Not something a good father would do.

He shrugged. "Papa keeps telling me no one's betting on me but...I dunno. He tells me he only wants me to win because he loves me and wants the best for me."

For the kid's sake, I hoped that was true. "Good," I said. "That's good, Giorgio." Better than my piece of shit old man, ironically.

"Pappa loves me," he said softly, with a little smile.

It was time to get back to a subject that didn't stir up all my old bitterness. "Listen, Giorgio, Randy has built you a mean machine. I went over it with a fine-tooth comb, and there's nothing I can do that would make it run any better. So, Goldilocks is great. You're great. Just fix your anxiety, okay, and kick ass out there."

"Is my dad paying you?" He looked concerned.

"Nope. I told you what the deal is." Ha, some *deal*. Extortion, yes. Deal? No.

"Well, he should pay you. I mean, you're a professional. It's not right."

"Forgiving my dad's debt will be payment enough," I said.

"If you say so." He drooped. "Anxiety is a real bummer."

"Fact, Giorgio. Every driver has anxiety. I had tons and I still won. You can, too."

He shook his head firmly. "You don't understand, Tony. It gets so bad I can't feel the steering wheel. What if I end up crashing? What if I kill another driver?" He was trembling now.

He lost sensation in his hands? That wasn't good. "How long does your anxiety last?"

"Until the finish line."

"Shit, that's bad, Giorgio."

He stared at the tarmac.

"All the more reason to call Dr. Hotz. Okay?"

"Okay," he said, distracted, then cried, "Hey, I've got an idea. Why don't we practice-race while I use Dr. Hotz's techniques?"

"You have more than one car?"

"I have five."

Five? At minimum, thirty grand each, that was a whole lot of fatherly love. "And Beppe won't mind?"

"Not if he thinks it will help me win."

"OK, we'll try it." If it gave him a chance to practice using Dr. Hotz's suggestions, it'd be worth it.

"But don't worry, if the doctor can't fix my anxiety, Randy says he can help me win. Although it's a little illegal."

He had a crazy look in his eyes, the same one I was sure was spinning behind Randy's sunglasses.

The hazard lights in my brain fired up.

He nodded frantically. "Randy's a genius. He's got a secret weapon. It's totally new science, he says." His pupils had dilated a little.

How delusional are you? A "secret weapon" designed by Randy Rocket could turn out to be a frickin' Doomsday Device.

"Look, Giorgio, we're not gonna use weird secret weapons or illegal methods or any of that shit. End of story."

He protested. "New science doesn't lie."

"Listen, Giorgio, you don't want to get disqualified. And my mother will be screwed. You gotta do this thing the right way." I realized I'd been shaking my fists.

I had nothing left for Giorgio's Daddy issues. Or his dependency on Randy. Hopefully, Dr. Hotz could help him with both things. But I did feel sorry for him. He looked so lost, and he was a nice kid.

"Where did you say you were from?" I said, trying to lighten the mood a little.

His eyes lit up. "Greensborough."

"I know that place. North of Cayuga on the Grand River, right? Lots of farmland out that way. And wild turkeys."

He laughed like a happy little kid. "Papa raised me up on a farm so I wouldn't grow up evil like the townie kids. And speaking of turkeys, Papa and me go hunting every spring. Got us a nice Tom this year. You should come with us some time."

"Maybe." Me and Beppe in the woods with guns? Bad idea. "Townies in Greensborough? Isn't there like six people living there?"

"I know, right?" He chuckled. "Papa's so overprotective. But that's because he loves me."

OK, this little kid act was getting on my nerves.

"So you still call your dad Papa?"

"Oh, he'll always be my Papa, even when I'm old and grey."

Part of me wished I could love my dad the way Giorgio loved his, the way I had as a kid—before Toto and Beppe ruined everything. My nerves were shot from this crazy day, so I called it quits.

"See you tomorrow," I said, climbing into the van. Giorgio waved and stepped up into his truck. Man, what wouldn't I have given to have a beautiful vintage ride like that, when I was his age? I'd been slogging away as a grease monkey, paying down a mortgage and raising kids.

Desperate for something normal, I pressed Alice Cooper into the CD player and cranked up the volume.

Dark fantasies of me blowing up the track and machine-gunning Beppe and his mobster buddies shelled my brain. I actually wondered if Donny knew a guy who could get me a machine gun? Then I gave myself a shake.

I tried to massage the stress out of my neck. It made the worst popping and cracking noises.

I realized that I'd matted my foot against the accelerator.

My tires screeched around a curve like wounded animals.

I realized I was barreling down a Highway to Hell, but not one of my own making. And there were no exit ramps!

"Fanculo!"

Chapter 9

I'd just finished my shift. The Price Chopper and Canadian Tire parking lot was bustled-up with shoppers and cars.

I had taken Angie's van today. Turns out my truck's transmission had bonked. That was specialty work beyond my capabilities. Transmission guys were in a league of their own. Plus, the work was expensive and the truck had a lot of miles on it, so I wasn't sure it was worth repairing. Until I knew what I wanted to do with it, I'd parked it in my driveway. I prayed my old racing pals didn't see me driving this van. *Oh how the mighty have fallen*, I could imagine them saying.

I swallowed an extra-strength ibuprofen and chased it down with water. I was medicating every day. Years of wrenching and osteoarthritis passed down through Dad (*thanks for the shitty genes, prick!*) had done a number on my fingers. They were crooked. And throbbed a lot. Sometimes I felt ashamed of them and hid them in my pockets. Last year, my left-hand pinky had called it quits. That had put a scare into me. But no matter, I wasn't about to trade my wrench in for a desk job. I'd rather jump off a cliff.

My Dad hadn't quit, either. By the time he'd hit fifty, his swollen fingers were like curved hockey stick blades and his knuckles had grown more knuckles. But, despite his pain and suffering, he'd found a way to keep working as a carpenter until he'd retired at sixty-five. I refused to be impressed. If he could last, I thought angrily, then so could I. In fact, I'd last a year longer, just to show him.

I was finally ready to know the truth. I whipped my phone out of the glovebox. I was hoping to get Ma, but Dad answered. He never knew who was calling because they still had an old rotary dial phone.

"Ma," I snapped. I didn't care that I was being rude.

Ma put her hand over the mouthpiece and sent him upstairs to the living room, where he'd sit on the plastic-covered couch reserved for guests and do "penance" (her words not mine) until we finished speaking and it was safe to come back down.

"How are you holding up, Ma?"

"As fine as God allows." Even after all these years in Canada, she still had God in her heart and Italy in her voice.

I couldn't say the hard thing first. So I said the easier thing. "Have you spoken to Angelina recently?"

"No," Ma said. "Why? What's going on?"

"She wants to take the bus. By herself."

"Good. It's about time."

"What? No, it's not! How old was I when I started taking the bus?"

"Eight, I think."

"Eight? Ma, that's way too young. What were you and Dad thinking?"

"Ah, parents worry too much these days! When you and Josie were young, we gave you freedom. On weekends and holidays, we'd send you outside and you played until dinner. After your homework and chores were done, of course. And you had scrapes and bruises and stories to tell. Nowadays, parents are too scared for their children and over-protect them. I hardly see kids out playing anymore. I'm sure there were diddlers around then, too, you know, but we didn't let it ruin our life." She went silent. "Is there something you need to tell me?"

"What? No, Ma, there isn't! I wasn't *diddled* as kid, okay. And I'm pretty sure Josie wasn't, either."

"Hm. This bus business isn't about Angelina," she said, quietly. "This is about you. You're afraid to let go of her."

She had me. As always. I sighed. "Maybe. But she's only ten."

Ma was silent.

"So, you think Angelina's old enough to take the bus to her swimming lesson?" I said. "I guess it's not that far. A short ride up Steel Street then a block's walk to the community center."

"Sure. Let her go. She runs fast like you did at her age. And she's strong-willed like you. Maybe wait with her at the bus stop when she leaves. Pick her up there, too. There's usually lots of people around. She'll be fine."

"Maybe. I'll talk it over with Angie. But I still think she's too young."

"Your little girl is growing up," Ma said. "They all do."

"Please don't say that."

"You're too overprotective, Tony. And you and I both know why."

We did—it had everything to do with Dad.

An old silence grew between us. The estrangement between Dad and me had done a real number on her.

I wondered if Ma knew about the debt but was pretending she didn't. She had a history of covering up for him.

"Something else is wrong, Tony, I can tell."

Ask it, man! Don't be a coward!

The words flew out of my mouth. "Ma, tell me the truth about Dad's mob connections. All of it. I need to know. I'm ready."

"You are?" she said softly.

"Guess I finally am."

Her voice got matter-of-fact. "Beppe Santucci ran the show. His business partner was Uncle Toto. But they weren't mafia. They were small-time gangsters, and they ran a gambling operation out of Little Italy Sports Bar on Barton Street. You could bet on anything. Beppe and Toto got rich, but Dad didn't. He got poor. He was addicted to gambling and was always in debt to them. If it wasn't for his carpentry skills, they would have turned him into fish food. So, after working all day building houses with Salvatore and Sons, he'd renovate tear-downs for Beppe and Toto so they could flip them for a profit. Oh, they made a small fortune. But Papa? Didn't get a cent. Even though he worked himself to the bone." She scoffed. "Some life, huh? So that's why your

Dad was rarely home. He was either out losing at the track or fixing up houses for those two thieves."

I had zero respect for Dad. It was his own fault he'd had to work his fingers to the bone.

"Sorry you married a friggin' loser, Ma."

"Watch your mouth, son! He's *my* loser, and I love him. And he's also your father, so don't talk about him like that. Gambling's an addiction, just like alcohol."

Sure. But Dad never tried to quit. An addict who ruined his family but never tried to quit? An asshole. "Tell me about Beppe." Speaking of assholes.

She snorted. "Big ego."

"And Toto?"

"Dangerous. They both were."

I was going to ask her more, but a part of me didn't want to know, in case I softened towards Dad. He didn't deserve my sympathy, addict or not.

"As a kid I knew they were dangerous," I said. "So I created this story in my head where Beppe kills Dad and everyone lives happily ever after."

Ma gasped. "Antonio! You didn't!"

"Only kidding, Ma! Relax!" Except I hadn't been kidding.

"What kind of son says that?" she cried. "Huh?"

I'd gone too far, but surely she of all people would understand why.

She fussed for a few minutes, then said, "What, you don't ask how your poor Ma's doing?"

Right then I knew she wasn't that mad at me.

Over the years, when there was tension between us, Ma would jokingly default to this shtick. The poor, neglected Italian mama. "Haha, Ma, very funny. Of course I know you're doing alright, otherwise you would have told me by now. Like always."

"You know me too well, son."

"I do."

We were good again. For a while, anyway.

"Love you, Ma."

"Love you, too, Tony."

I was about to hang up when she said, "Tony, I didn't want to tell you so much at once. But you needed to hear it. You're going to handle this properly, now, like a grown man."

Whatever that meant! I tried not to feel pissed off at her. "Maybe. Bye, Ma." I hung up fast.

Her words rang in my head. Maybe Dad's debts weren't all his fault. He was an addict. Still, that didn't let him off the hook for wrecking our family.

Violent images throttled inside my head: Toto torturing Angie and Angel if Giorgio lost, Ma living in a shit hole eating dog food out of a can, Dad on a street corner begging for change, then throwing his nickels on a bet at the Little Italy Sports Club. Like a real addict.

For the first time ever, I felt sorry for him—Ma had put a chink in my armour. *Dammit, Ma!*

Chapter 10

ONE PROVEN WAY FOR me to forget my own bullshit was hearing the guys spew theirs, which, until recently, had always been way worse and way more interesting than mine, so when Donny rang me at home and invited me to Tim's, I was relieved.

So, there we were, at our table, early evening, John and Norb and me, three knuckleheads waiting for Donny-Come-Lately.

That night we were stuck in reverse, eating and drinking in silence. Usually, we did that after someone spilled his guts, like our version of a celebration dinner. That particular Tim Hortons coffee shop had seen a lot of crazy crap, thanks to us.

Once, after Donny attended Karl The Magician's mind-reading seminar, he'd tried to guess our thoughts. He'd failed, of course, and we had laughed our asses off, but Donny was pissed off. He was convinced that eventually he'd prove us wrong. We were still waiting.

Another time, Norb had embarrassed the crap out of me when he'd showed up with his Magic 8 Ball. Paul Woodley, one of my work buddies, had been waiting in line for his coffee. He smirked at me like a real a-hole. I tried to get Norb to cool it with the toy, but he ignored me. When Norb gets on a roll, I think his brain shuts out everything else. Next thing I knew, Paul had strolled over to watch and we ended up taking turns shaking the ball. We were all howling with laughter. Then John asked the ball if Donny was going to put on a second Making Steven Famous concert, and the ball said "yes"! Donny went the colour of plaster dust. Paul asked for a turn. He asked the ball if me and my buddies were retards, and the ball said "signs point to yes". That was the end of *that* fun time.

Now, Donny finally burst through the main doors.

"Totally fucking unbelievable!" he cried, making his way to the counter with as much drama as possible. He even did a weird little twirl when he came back to our table, like some kind of magician doing a big reveal. Donny was definitely full of tricks—mostly fucked-up ones.

He plunked a box of sour cream glazed donuts on the table. "Help yourselves, boys!" he cried. He fished one out and chomped on it.

He was firing on all cylinders. I hadn't seen him this amped for awhile, and that worried me, because this was a guy who'd completely demolished his own life when he was in a maniac mood.

He leaned forward. "So, I walked out my door to go pick up the garbage cans, and I see this old beater parked across the street. The guy behind the wheel is staring at me and taking notes of some kind. And he's wearing these *huge*, wonky sunglasses. Guess who it was?"

"Here we go," John said.

Norb was intrigued, of course. "CSIS? No, wait, it wasn't the Candid Camera guy, was it? Peter Funt?"

"What?" Donny said, thrown off for a moment. "No, it was that friggin' Dave Walker. But when I booted down my driveway to introduce myself, he burned rubber."

"That's too bad," Norb said sadly. "It would have been cool to be on Candid Camera."

I was fed up with Donny's Walker stories.

"Why would Walker stalk you?" I said, sounding maybe just a tiny bit annoyed. "You think you see him everywhere."

Donny shrugged and stuffed half a donut into his mouth. His cheeks puffed out like a chipmunk's.

"Maybe he's writing a story about you." Leave it to John to turn this nutty topic into some kinda theory. "I mean, you wrote about Steven, so maybe now Walker's writing about *you*." He crossed his legs and bobbed his foot. He looked really pleased with his analysis.

"Writing a story about me?" Donny laughed. "Now there's a guaranteed fail. But wait! There's more!" And there he was, like an infomercial salesman, once again about to pitch a bonus gift! Lucky us!

"Yesterday, I was in the food court at the mall eating a cheeseburger and I looked up and saw Walker standing beside the lottery booth, filming me with this old-fashioned Super 8 camera."

"Woah, diddly!" Norb was impressed.

"Oh yeah Norb, and do you remember that cool Rush t-shirt he used to wear?"

"No," John said flatly. "Why would we?"

"Well Buster Brown, he was wearing that *same* t-shirt, but it was in mint condition! And he looked exactly as he did in Grade 13! He hadn't aged!"

Norb's jaw hung open. "I've heard of this kind of thing," he whispered.

"When he saw me looking at him, he took off. You should have seen the way he dodged people! Like a running back! It was mind-blowing."

I closed my eyes. How many times had Donny brought up this idiot's name over the years?

"Gimme a break. Walker was a total *forgettable*," I said. "And why the frick would he film you? Why would *anyone* film you, Donny? It's usually the other way around—you filming someone else, like Norb."

Remembering his horrible time as the Village Vigilante and Humpty-Dumpty, which was the direct result of Donny's video nonsense, Norb nervously bit his lip. I gave him a little pat on the shoulder. *Donny, you owe Norb a lifetime of apologies!*

"Next time you see Walker filming you, call the cops," I said to Donny. "And press charges. If he is filming you, the guy's obviously a nutjob stalker." Then I felt bad for saying that—John had just got through a bad spell where he essentially stalked his ex, Sophia.

"Wait, there's more!" Donny cried. "After the incident at the mall, I went down to his house and stalked *him* with my camera. Ha-ha! Touché, motherfucker!"

"Do you think that was a good idea?" Norb gasped. "What if you got caught and ended up going to jail? Or what if Walker was filming you filming him filming you?" His eyes widened. "What an evil genius."

"What were you trying to accomplish, Love?" I asked, ignoring Norb.

"This is going to sound crazy," Donny said, "but—"

John gave me the "Doesn't it always?" look.

"—but it's come to my attention that Walker has discovered the secret to happiness."

Norb actually covered his mouth with his hands.

"Yep. He plays guitar all day long. Listens to jazz albums. And he lives in a super small but nice house. A nice, tight life." He slurped his coffee. "I'd killed for a life like that."

"That's it?" Norb looked disappointed. "I thought it was going to be more magical than that."

"How do you know what Walker does all day?" I asked.

Donny avoided my gaze. There was my answer.

I was best pals with two stalkers and a child in a man's body. No surprises there.

"You're obsessed with Walker," John said. "I ought to know, right? It's a sickness, buddy. You can't fix it on your own. See Dr. Hotz or you're going to end up in jail. End of story, to quote Tony." His face was a little red, but he met our eyes.

Donny just laughed John off.

"John's right," Norb said sheepishly. "Stalking's bad, Donny. And I hear jail's a horrible place."

John said, "Anyway, you know Walker's happiness is an illusion, right, Donny? I mean, he might be happy sometimes, but not necessarily any happier than you or me or anyone else. Surely, you can see that?"

"Are you sure you got the right house?" I asked.

"Yes," Donny said, hurt. "I absolutely did! I've seen him go in there." His eyes were flicking around, his thoughts obviously ping-ponging.

"What about you, Tony?" John asked, changing the subject. Trying to fix Donny was getting us nowhere. "How bad are things at the track?"

"Yeah, Tone," Donny said. "Spill, brother." I could tell he was glad to be out of the hot seat for a while.

I gave them the latest gangster update from Hermonville Raceway, but again left out the crazy Randy stuff. I just wasn't up to talking about it.

"Walker was the rubber man extraordinaire," Donny said, sadly. "There wasn't a situation he couldn't handle, or one he couldn't create and escape from when it was time. In a few short years, he'd basically taught me how to live the rest of my life."

What the eff? We were still talking about this ridiculous topic? "I remember him in gym class wrestling," I said, "and only once did I ever see him rubber out from a guy. The rest of the time he got creamed." I'd just told these guys about my real-life troubles, but all they could do was spew off about Dave Walker?

"You got it wrong, Tony," Norb said. "Walker *was* a rubber man. After school one day, I saw him show up at a football practice and get into it with Dale Miller! You remember him? Quarterback? Walker called him out in front his team mates for being a jock asshole, and that pissed Miller off, so to save face he ran over and tackled Walker and started pummelling him. But every time Dale tried to land a punch, Walker squirmed just enough to avoid getting hit. Dale went nuclear. Then, like Houdini, Walker squeaked out from under him and somersaulted to his feet." Norb licked his chops. "You guys won't believe what happened next?"

"Spill," John said, despite himself.

Donny was on the edge of his seat.

Norb's eyes were like saucers. "Walker started chanting, *this little piggy went to the market, this little piggy stayed home, this little piggy had roast beef, this little piggy had none, and this little piggy went, wee, wee, wee, all the way home!'* Then he started tickling Miller! There must have been a hundred kids watching and laughing their butts off. It was the darndest thing. Miller was so freaked out, but Walker was already all the way across the field before Miller thought to run after him. Lucky if Miller ran even twenty yards before he gave up."

Donny looked almost jealous.

"And—" Norb paused.

"For the love of God Norb, what?" I yelled. I was barely holding on.

He rubbed his hands together with great delight. "The next day Miller snuck up behind Walker, threw him against his locker and punched him in the face."

"Hmph," I shrugged. "Sounds about right."

Norb looked troubled. "But you know what else? Walker just laughed as if Miller had told him a funny. Even though the blood just gushed out of his nose."

"What the hell?" John said. "This is the first I'm hearing of this."

"Then what happened?" Donny asked. He was almost shaking. Hearing that his hero had had a nosebleed was too much.

"I can't remember," Norb said, pale as paper. "And I don't want to."

"I knew Miller was a jerk," John said, "but not violent. Sorry you had to see that, buddy. That must have really messed you up."

Norb nodded sadly.

"But in fairness to Miller," I said, "Walker was a jerk, too. If he'd kept his mouth shut Dale would have left him alone. Walker *knew* what he was doing."

"It's almost as if Walker *wanted* Miller to punch him out, so he'd be stuck with the guilt for the rest of his life, so in the end Walker would win." Donny was twisting this story around, desperate to hang on to his delusion.

"Well then, Walker really was an asshole," I said, "and lucky to be alive. Miller could've killed him if he'd wanted to."

"This is a true story, right, Norb?" I said, searching the guys' faces, "Not a made-up one, like the Steeltown Avenger?"

"Swear on Mutti's grave it is," he said, crossing himself.

For once, Donny had the good sense to change the subject. Norb was looking pretty shaken.

"Tell us more about the porn star actor, Tony," Donny said.

I could tell he was referring to Randy Rocket.

John snorted and Norb's cheeks turned pink.

So, I told them about Randy's crazy shenanigans.

Donny sputtered coffee out of his mouth. "The guy's insane! And are you sure it isn't Walker pretending to be Randy? That sounds exactly like something he'd do!"

"Yeah, numb nuts," I said, angrily, "like you'd know what Walker would do. And can we please get off this ridiculous obsession with him?"

"How can you say something that Walker would have done," John said to Donny. "Who even knows what Walker's like now? Or what he'd do in any situation? It's all guesswork. And why would you even put in the effort?"

Donny slumped. "Yeah, yeah, I know. I'm pathetic. Donny this, Donny that. And now listen to him, he's talking about himself in the third person."

"Look, it really is Randy Rocket, OK, Love," I said. "He looks exactly like he did working Nascar, just a little older. And I've talked to him about past races and cars he's worked on and he remembers all of it. So he's definitely who he says he is."

"I dunno, Tony," Donny said, "Patricia's pretty good, and I know guys who are quick studies. They'd master Randy's M.O. in a flash."

I really didn't want to talk about his nutty Incognito group and their love of disguises. Man, my buddy was obsessive. I shoved his shoulder, totally fed up.

He laughed, unfazed.

"What are you going to do about Randy, Tony?" Norb asked. He was using that scared five-year-old voice that came out when he was especially anxious. I could appreciate that—hell, I was anxious, too, but if he didn't stop, I'd smack him.

Donny suddenly sprang to his feet, jabbing his finger towards someone. "Guys! It's him. It's Walker!"

In the far corner of the coffee shop, sitting at a two-seater by himself was a man wearing a Rush t-shirt and clownish sunglasses. Not a stitch of a lie, it was Dave Walker, and the fucker was filming us!

I barged out of my chair, upending it. A young girl at a table beside us shrieked.

"Turn that friggin' thing off," I shouted.

Donny was already sprinting toward the guy. "Dave Walker!" he cried, "it's me, Donny Love from Irondale!" The poor idiot was star-struck! What the fuck?

"No one films me without my friggin' permission!" I roared, charging at Walker.

The patrons had gone silent, preparing to witness a murder.

His Super 8 camera still glued to his eye, Walker bumped out of his seat—he was taller than I remembered him.

He grabbed a file storage box off his table and arced it through the air, showering Donny and me and an old couple at the table with God knows what. Then he whipped his chair toward my legs to trip me up and ran outside, fast as a jack rabbit.

We chased after him out into the parking lot, but the fucker was greased lightning. Loose-limbed and wonky, he dove feet-first through his open car window and burned rubber out onto Molson Boulevard, through a red light.

"Fuck you!" I cried, shaking. Even I could see that the degree of rage I was feeling was out of proportion.

Donny and John were slack-jawed. And Norb was so messed up he was rocking back and forth.

In stunned silence we went back inside to see just what Walker had flung at us. We gathered it all up off the floor, stuffed it in his box, and set it down at his table.

Norb looked like a kid digging into his Christmas stocking as he fished out an old combination lock and lovingly admired it. "Cool, I bet this was Walker's from Irondale."

Then he pulled out a nub of pink eraser, a desk splinter, a dirty sweat sock, pictures Walker had obviously cut out of our Grade Nine yearbook, and, God knows why, photos of the Tartan Club, the Germania Club, the Italian Club and also our childhood homes.

Donny reached in and reverently took out a Three Dog Night album I'd loved so much, *Harmony*. Behind it was BTO's *Not Fragile*, another classic.

"It's like some kind of time capsule," Donny said.

"Maybe he was on his way to bury it," Norb said.

"A *cardboard* time capsule?" I said.

"No one walks around with a big box of memorabilia," Donny said. "And he chose to throw it at us, so he obviously wanted us to see this stuff. The question is why?"

"It's all very strange," John said. "He's obviously got psychiatric issues."

"Maybe he's like you, Donny," Norb said. "He carries his past around with him."

Donny glared at him. "That's old news, Norb. Anyway, I'm working on it, as you well know." That was true—he'd always been open about his struggles. And he'd pulled us all into those struggles more than once.

Norb gave him an apologetic smile.

Donny's brain suddenly popped. "Negative attention! That's it! Walker *wanted* us to see him filming us and he *wanted* us to see the memorabilia and he wanted us to be pissed off at him so we'd chase him, and—"

"If that's true, then he's a worse fucking attention-seeker than you, Love," I cried, shaking my head. "After I kill him, you're next!"

"Language!" Elise, the shift manager warned from behind the counter. She was a tough old bird and ran a tight ship.

"Sorry, Elise," we said in unison.

"We'll get Walker," John said, looking positively thrilled by the challenge. "We'll find a way. And then we'll put an end to his bullshit once and for all."

Donny said, "You're right about him being an attention-seeker, Tony. He's way worse than me. And that's really saying something because I am the worst."

Norb and John bobbed their heads in agreement.

I'd never felt so fucked up and vulnerable and violated and powerless. Walker seemed dangerous to me. On the way home, I was going to buy a security system and install it right away.

And I'd give Angie and Angel strict orders not to leave the house until they checked the cameras. Walker could be filming us behind our maple tree, or under our porch, or under our friggin' beds!

And the added bonus of a security system would be protection against Beppe and his thugs. Shit, suddenly my life was full of dangerous criminals and nutbars!

My body seemed to be vibrating. *Don't let him get to you. If you survived Donny, you can survive Walker. He's twice the idiot Donny is. For now, just focus on Giorgio's win. Deal with Walker later.*

My phone rang and I just about jumped out of my skin.

It was Randy. "Goldilock's broken. Tire specs ding-donged. Engine blew. Universe must be angry. Come now. Hurry. Clippity-clop!"

"Clippity-clop, Randy?" I snapped, "and you want me to come now?" I checked my watch. "It's eight o'clock? Can't it wait until tomorrow?"

His answer was to hang up.

"You okay, Tone?" John asked carefully. He was eyeballing me like I'd sprouted horns.

I was too full of anxiety and frustration to answer him. I gave the boys a half-hearted explanation and headed out. I had to work on Randy's terms. For Ma's sake. As I walked outside past the main window, Norb and Donny were still busy scouring the floor for anything they'd missed.

To say I was steaming mad at Walker would have been a colossal understatement. When I got a hold of him, I'd one-hundred percent tear him a new one!

I climbed into my van, glancing at the clock on the dash.

Guilt slammed me. On top of not taking Angel to her swimming lessons, I hadn't tucked her in. That had *never* happened before. Suddenly, I felt like a deadbeat father. The way my dad would have felt when I was a kid—if he'd had a conscience, that is.

Chapter 11

AN HOUR LATER, I WAS stomping through the raceway clubhouse and onto the track. I'd called Angie to tell her I'd be late getting home, and she'd cussed out the mafia bastards and told me not to take any of their shit.

Moths swarmed through the fluorescent light coming from the light standards. Twilight was on its way out.

Giorgio was in our pit with Beppe and the boys. *Shit!* They paid zero attention to Randy, who was hunched over Goldilock's engine, singing "Hush Little Baby, Don't Say a Word". Of course he was! Why wouldn't he be?

Predictably, the stands were empty.

When I got closer, I realized the idiots and the crooks were having a jolly conversation about the Hamilton Tiger Cats' glory days.

"...Garney Henley was the best wide receiver ever to play the game," Beppe said, waving his fat cigar in the air, throwing a whole lotta' Godfather into his voice.

Toto stabbed the air with *his* stogie. "But don't forget Angelo Mosca. Best defensive lineman to grace the field."

Beppe fake-jabbed Giorgio. Giorgio bobbed and weaved, protecting his face with his dukes, laughing playfully as if enjoying a familiar routine with his sweet, shitbag Nonno.

"Man, I wished I'd grown up in the Garney era," Doughboy said. "Life was better then." He snapped his fingers to nail home his point. What a suck-up.

Beppe's face hardened. "You're full of shit, Elio! The old days were horrible. Things are better now. You don't know how good you got it!"

Doughboy shut his mouth. Whatever the boss said was law, I guess.

Uncle Toto cried, "Tony's here! Evviva!"

Beppe clapped his hands and rubbed them together, like he was going to eat me for dinner.

Everyone was happy-looking. But not me. I had my angry bulldog face on, and I was fantasizing about taking bocce balls to all their skulls.

For some nutbar reason (was there any other), Randy felt it necessary to belt out, "Night Time Is The Right Time".

"Ray Charles, *again*?" Doughboy said. "Don't you know anything else?" He smirked at the others but found they were all spellbound by Randy.

He was bent over the hood lovingly stroking what I hoped was the engine. It was hard to tell.

When I went over to take a look, my gut dropped into my boots. "Where's the friggin' engine, Randy?"

"Told you already. Wrong tire specs. Over-revved the engine. Broken Valve." He shook his head sadly. "My fault. Universe spoke. Randy ignored 'er. Bad Randy." He gave his bum a smack.

Then he pointed to the back of the pit stop. Laid out on a huge tarp was the car's 360 Kistler engine—in pieces! Beside it was a huge red tool drawer on wheels, a portable workbench, and a hydraulic hoist.

"You said the problem was a broken valve! So why did you tear the engine apart? That doesn't make sense. You of all people should know that!"

He faced me, his jaw jutting out angrily. "Just a routine dispersal. Gotta get rid of those electromagnetic waves. Fresh start."

I was beside myself. What the hell did electromagnetism have to do with anything?

"The knower knows!" Randy barked. "So break it down. Rebuild it. *Bing-bang-bong!* Can you dig it?"

"No, Randy, I can't *dig it! You* chose to tear the engine apart, so *you* put it back together. Why should I clean up your mess?"

"He's got a point," Uncle Toto said, nodding philosophically.

Randy jittered into my personal space, all energized and angry. "Broke it down *blind*, padre. Me." He poked his chest. "Master."

The fools around me looked like they were silently agreeing with Randy.

"Could've made *you* take it apart, Grasshopper," he said. "But I didn't. Show Tony some love, I told myself. Damn right. So I did. Big time."

"Bullshit." *Grasshopper, my ass.*

"One: know the engine. Two: know the driver. Three: driver wins. End of story."

"End of story? That's my fucking line, Randy, not yours, so take it back!"

"You can't copyright a saying."

"I'm not putting the friggin' engine back together. It will take all night."

"Goldilocks needs you. Giorgio needs you." He blew a kiss at the disaster on the tarp, then shuffled off like a drifter leaving town.

I kicked at the dirt. Man, I know I was acting like an eight-year-old.

The gangsters were shoe-gazing. Had our spat embarrassed them?

"Randy!" I shouted after him.

"Ha! Useless as a glass hammer!" he shouted over his shoulder. Then he started speed-walking, his hips jutting side-to-side.

"How about I take a glass hammer to your skull," I grumbled to myself.

For the first time since we'd been married, I wouldn't be in bed with Angie tonight, and that made me feel unbelievably lonely. My wife would understand, but I knew I'd let her down, her and my little Angel.

"I'll help you put Goldilocks back together," Giorgio offered cheerfully. "I'm really good at passing tools."

I sank. He'd basically said he was totally useless.

"Hey," Beppe said, "we will all help." Everyone nodded, including Doughboy. What a champ, wanting to help out ol' Tony. The thought of those three crooks "helping" me made me sick, but what choice did I have, really?"

Toto grinned at all of us. "I'll order a couple of pies from Gino's Pizza. Team effort, right Beppe?"

Well, wasn't that just swell? We were going to have a pizza party, me and my new pals.

Beppe got all dramatic again, hand over his heart. "If it be now, 'tis not to come: if it be not to come, it will be now: if it be now, yet it will come: the readiness is all."

I figured it was friggin' Shakespeare again. What a diva.

Toto applauded Beppe. "Brilliant, Beppe. Bravo!" Like Beppe was Robert De Niro or something.

Alice Cooper was wailing "No More Mr. Nice Guy" on a loop in my head. I wanted to smack that gold-toothed smile right off of Toto's weaselly face. A pipe inside me burst.

"I will fix this fucker," I shouted, "but I work alone! The last thing I need is a bunch of amateurs leaning over my shoulder. All of you just need to hit the friggin' road! Now!"

"Ahi!" Beppe cried. "So sensitive."

I just glared at him. I was afraid that, if I opened my trap, I'd end up saying some things that could get me into real trouble. Yeah, they were idiots, but I had no doubt they knew how to pull a damn trigger.

But instead of being pissed at me, Beppe and the other two dirtbags fell in with each other and headed down the track towards the clubhouse, joking and laughing, probably about the time they gave some poor guy cement shoes.

I reminded myself that they were only jolly because things were going their way. If Giorgio lost, then what? They might force me to work for them full-time, for free. They'd basically done that to Dad. And if I refused, then what? I shuddered, thinking of my family. I wondered what kind of threats they'd made against Ma and Josie and me, all those years ago.

"Have a great night, guys!" Giorgio shouted to the merry mobsters.

"You too, bro," Doughboy called back. "We should go bowling again!"

"You're on!" Giorgio said.

I imagined Mob Night at Irondale Lanes. Suddenly, I was thinking I wasn't going to take my kid bowling anymore. Not if there was even a *chance* that Doughboy might be in the next lane.

Then I noticed that Dad was in the stands.

He grinned and waved at Giorgio, like they knew each other well.

I felt a jab of jealousy, which made me angry. Hey, Giorgio can be your *new* son Dad, I thought bitterly. After all, you didn't raise him and disappoint the fuck out of him. He doesn't know the real you.

I stared meat cleavers at him as he came down the stairs and onto the track. Lucky for him, not once did he look at me. When he caught up with the mobsters, they welcomed him with open arms and back-slapping.

As if *they* were his real family.

Fueled by rage and fear, I began the process of re-building the engine. I hated Randy for putting me through this. He knew I was a damn good mechanic, that I wasn't some kid who couldn't tell the difference between a carburetor and a piston.

Giorgio was so kind to me that I didn't have the heart to tell him to hit the road. He'd set up portable lights and we started doing a quicky inventory of all the parts lined up on the tarp.

He seemed to enjoy learning about the intricacies of his engine, and he was actually really good at handing me tools, so I could tell he'd been around them. Maybe he'd done a bit of work on tractors at the family farm. At one point, I asked him for a left-handed screwdriver and he'd caught the joke right away. In his own way, the kid was alright.

Man, that engine was a beauty. All the components were top-notch. Randy had cleaned and machined every piece. It was a pleasure to work on an eight-cylinder engine. Being a 410, I figured that we might be able to get her up to 900 horsepower—to a car nut like me, the thought of it was mind-blowing. What would it feel like, to be behind the wheel of a fireball like that?

"Break time," Giorgio said, after a couple of hours, patting me on the back. He went over and hauled out four big-ass sausages and two ice-cold Cokes from a cooler, then fired up a table-top BBQ he'd placed on the portable workbench. I pressed the Coke can against my head, and sighed with pleasure.

After wolfing down the sausages, we got back to work. I felt like I was really getting a feel for the car. Damn him, Randy had been right.

There were some modifications that made no sense, though. For one thing, the left and right wings were placed oddly, with higher wing angles.

Giorgio saw me eyeballing them. "Randy did that. Gives me much better down force. Amazing traction and so much better on the turns."

But the thing that threw me was how Randy had modified the hood. When I went to fit it over the engine, there was a fairly large gap it and the injector stacks. I looked over at Giorgio.

"Don't ask," he said. "I'm not allowed to tell."

Great. More kookiness. I didn't have the energy to press him.

When we'd finished running the car through some test-laps, it was two in the morning, and I was friggin' beat. If we won, I'd tell Randy his engine was a work of art.

"When do you see Dr. Hotz?" I asked Giorgio.

"Tomorrow morning."

"Nervous?" He sure looked it

"Yes sir."

"Don't be. You'll be fine. You are going, right?"

"Of course," he said as earnest as a Boy Scout. "Anything for Papa."

And there it was again. His desperate, childish need to please Beppe. But I was too tired to pry. It was none of my business, anyway.

"Today's going to be a write-off at work," I yawned. "Lucky if I'll get four hours of sleep."

"Same," Giorgio said. "I have to get up at six to clean out the henhouse, just me and the chickens!" He looked happy at the prospect.

"Thanks for helping me, Giorgio. You're a good assistant. But don't quit your day job."

"Hah, good one, Tony."

We said our goodbyes in the parking lot. I was about to drive off when I got that weird prickly feeling in the back of my neck. I swear I felt eyes on me. Nervous as hell, I scanned the parking lot for Walker.

But there was no sign of him, but it didn't mean that he wasn't there.

In high school, Walker had been beige. Boring. Barely noticeable.

He hadn't played on any school teams, acted in any plays, been in the school band, gotten in a fight, showed up stoned, raised his hand in class, or mouthed off to a teacher. He was always sitting alone in the cafeteria at lunch time.

I would have felt sorry for Walker, but not now. He'd fucked with my privacy. For all I knew, he'd been filming my family. That's when my brain shut down. Between mafia extorting me and crazy Walker stalking me and my friends, I felt like I might lose my marbles.

I fish-tailed out of the lot.

When I burned rubber out onto the deserted highway, the passenger side tires caught air. Instead of righting the van, I released the wheel to see what would happen, knowing full well it might go all the way over.

When the van bumped back down onto all four wheels, I had to pull over and put it in Park for a minute. My hands were shaking.

Maybe insanity was contagious.

Chapter 12

It was family movie night.

I'd ordered in Angel's favourite—double cheese and pepperoni—from Aurora Pizzeria, but before we picked it up, we hit the grocery store. For Angel, we bought salt and vinegar chips, sour cherry candy and lemonade. And for Angie and me, macaroons and dill pickle chips. We picked up a six pack of Coors Lite from the Beer Store.

After all that tasty junk, we were pleasantly bagged out in the family room watching *Shrek 2,* and so far I hadn't fallen asleep, so Angel was happy about that.

But as the movie progressed, my brain kept going back to all my troubles, and I was almost grateful when Randy called. I took the call in the kitchen, so I wouldn't interrupt the talking donkey.

Apparently, King Beppe wanted me back at the track, pronto. My back went right up, and I tried to argue with Randy. But it was like banging my head against a wall. Finally, I lost it completely.

"I don't care if Giorgio has a surprise for me! Tell Beppe to fuck off!" I bellowed before I hung up.

When I stomped back into the family room, the movie was paused. Angie looked pissed off.

Angel had crossed her arms over her chest. "Dad, we heard that," she scolded. "Don't swear. Next time you swear, I'll swear, too."

I felt like a real bastard. I mean, I swore a lot, but *never* in front of the kids, and especially not in front of my little girl. What had come over me? This was all because of the pressure-cooker of trying to keep Ma from losing her home. And *that* was all my Dad's fault.

"I'm really sorry I swore, honey," I said to Angel. "I know dads aren't supposed to do that. Can you forgive me? I promise I won't let it happen again."

I could tell she didn't believe me. She'd probably heard it a thousand times a day at school but this was her father who'd said it, and in a red-hot, yelling rage, too.

I hauled my ass out the door, feeling like the saddest excuse for a father.

The apple hadn't fallen far from the tree, after all.

• • • •

DRIVING TO THE RACEWAY, something unexpected happened. At the intersection of Rymal Road and Highway 6, I found myself feeling giddy, like when I was a teen on the way to race. The feeling came out of nowhere. For once, instead of feeling guilty about it, like I normally did with all things racing, I welcomed it. It was the first bit of real joy I'd felt in many days. When the light turned green, I floored it and broke the speed limit by more than any father ever should.

And I decided I was going to enjoy Giorgio's surprise—no matter how stupid or bizarre it was likely to be—and then I was going to head back home to be with my family. And if anyone had a problem with that, then they could kiss my ass!

I started laughing like a madman and slapping the steering wheel. Something in my brain had popped. The pressure to win and all the bullshit that went with it had me riding the crazy train.

Next thing I knew, I was in the pit, plopped down at a card table with Randy and Giorgio, chomping on BBQ wings and garlic bread.

Giorgio said he was going to do the big reveal after we ate. I did my best to pretend I cared.

I was wearing a brand-new racing suit in fire-engine red. Giorgio had given it to me when I'd screeched into the parking lot. It was swell, to use his word. I didn't look half-bad in it. And to show him how grateful I was, I did a little jig for him.

He was sleek in his blue one.

Randy went through an elaborate inspection of each and every chicken wing before he'd eat it. He'd sniff it repeatedly, then examine it from all angles, then lick the BBQ sauce off. Then he'd put the entire wing in his mouth, chew loudly, and spit the bones out.

No wonder the big leagues had booted him. He was bonkers. After this upcoming race, he'd be lucky to find a job repairing slot cars

Around nine o'clock, just as I was wiping the stickiness off my face, I finally looked around at the rest of the raceway.

Further down the pit lane, beside a fire truck, ambulance, tow-truck, and the pick-up truck with equipment for oil spill clean-up, a bunch of first responders were playing cards.

The push-and-rescue driver's hair was teased up high. He looked like Jareth from *Labyrinth*, Angel's favourite movie. I liked Bowie's music, but, fashion-wise, he was a bit of a weirdo. *But then who wasn't these days?* I asked myself.

The EMT's head was shaved, and the firefighter was pretty clean-cut, too, but the tow-truck driver looked just like Hetfield. He was even wearing a Metallica t-shirt.

On the ground beside them, their boom box was blasting Def Leppard.

When they spotted me, the ambulance guy suddenly shot to his feet. "Holy shit! Guys! Look who it is!"

They all dropped their cards and hustled down the track towards me.

I braced myself. I guess that, for people who've never been hero-worshipped, the idea of fans drooling over you sounds sweet, but I absolutely hated it. All of it. The worst part was that guys like these guys thought there was something special or magical or whatever about me. What a load of BS.

Randy kept eating, totally disinterested. Maybe he wasn't as crazy as I'd thought.

The responders stopped in front of me in a semi-circle, eyebrows up in their frickin' hairlines.

"Prodigy," Hetfield panted. His eyes threatened to power-chord out of their sockets.

"Not anymore," I grunted.

"I saw you the other day but I didn't wanna bother you," he continued. "But today I thought what the hell, man, I'm gonna go over and ask the Prodigy for his autograph." There was a suspicious bit of moisture in his eyes. Was he getting ready to bawl over me?

"I'm such a huge fan," ambulance guy said.

"Yeah," said firefighter, "we talk about you all the time."

"You were the greatest," Ambulance guy said. He whipped out a racing program and a pen. "I'd be so honoured to get your autograph." He huffed. "Man, I'd give my left nut to be you. You had it all."

Giorgio looked spellbound by this whole ridiculous scene.

Whoever was driving the crazy train kicked me off. I was just feet-of-clay Tony, fucked-up and desperate, wedged between a rock and a hard place.

On the front page of the racing program there was a photo of me twenty years younger, long-haired and grinning like an idiot, hoisting a trophy. The headline shouted, "Hamilton's Racing Prodigy wins the Hermonville Special!"

I'd won ten grand in prize money in the last race. Angie and I had freaked out with excitement. We were rich! That dough paid the down payment on our house. That win had given us a great start in life. And then I'd quit.

I'd been so damn determined to be the man my dad hadn't been that I'd given up the thing that had felt like my destiny. That guy was right. I *had* had it all. I suddenly realized just how sick I was of trying not to repeat my father's mistakes.

I forced myself to scribble my signature on the guy's program "Don't go selling it in on Ebay," I said, trying to joke and feeling like a complete idiot.

"Are you kidding me? This baby is going into a frame," he said. "I promise."

I turned to go, but the push-and-rescue driver froze me in my tracks when he asked, "Why'd you quit, man?"

He'd unintentionally hit me where it hurt. "It's a long story, boys." They waited for a better answer. "My barber always said you can't put an old head on young shoulders, and he's right." I shrugged, barely able to look at them anymore.

Giorgio saw me squirm. Like a celebrity handler, he slid in between us and firmly asked them to leave. I didn't think he'd had it in him.

"Thanks, buddy," I said to Giorgio, after they'd gone. I was really touched that he'd rescued me like that.

"Aw, shucks, anything for you Tony." He sighed. "Honestly, I don't know what got into them asking you such a rude question. They're usually swell." He snapped his fingers, his smile back on his face. "Well, at least they got to meet their hero, right?"

"I'm no hero."

He gasped. "Don't you dare say that. You're *my* hero, okay? And you're your daughter's hero, too. And you're a hero to your old fans and rightly so. You were miraculous behind the wheel."

This chat was way too emotional for me, so when the gang down the lane cranked up "Born to be Wild", I could have French-kissed the fuckers.

"See, Tony," Giorgio said, "they *are* swell guys." Those swell guys were air-guitaring up a storm, singing at the top of their lungs. Giorgio smiled wide at everyone.

But then he grabbed his crotch. "Aw shoot! Gotta pee! Be right back!" He hobbled away toward the club house.

I sucked in a few deep breaths and tried to get my head back on straight. The past was the past. I was a different man now, and I had a great life, a great family.

But then I saw Dad up in the stands with those three devils, yukking it up, having a grand-old time.

I short-circuited. *You assholes! You have the gall to be friggin' merry after sticking me in a pressure cooker?*

If I'd had a machine-gun in my hand, I would have used it. Angie would have to get used to me in orange coveralls. Suddenly, from behind me, Giorgio cried, "Surprise, Birthday Boy!"

I whirled around.

On the track apron, next to Goldilocks, was another kick-ass 360 sprint car. Giorgio waved excitedly behind the wheel and shut off the engine. Randy had push-started him with his truck and was getting out.

So, this was the surprise he'd called me about? What the frig?

Giorgio leapt out, grabbed my arm, and corralled me over to it.

"It's not my birthday, Giorgio."

"I know, silly. But let's just pretend it is."

"Why?"

Giorgio looked at me earnestly. "Dr. Hotz said we should practice-race together, said it will help me overcome my anxiety. So, I got us another car."

"What does Dr. Hotz know about car racing?"

"You'd be surprised. Did you know that she's on the raceway board of directors? She's a huge racing fan and her daughter's a micro sprint driver."

"I did not know that," I said, but I'd only half-heard him. The gleaming white beauty in front of me had possessed me. Its red nose and top wing glowed like a candy apple. I found myself caressing the hood. The state-of-the-art Kistler engine made the hair on my arms stand up, and I swear I was falling head-over-heels in love.

"You know I don't race anymore, right? Besides, I drove mini stock, not one of these powerhouses." I shook my head. To race it would be thrilling. But I wasn't going to go there. I was fighting a powerful urge to climb inside it and just tear around the track.

"Dr. Hotz said that if we practice-race while she treats me, there's an excellent chance I'll break my second-place curse."

"She said that?"

"Darn tootin' she did!"

"Okay, Jethro."

"Good one, Tony!" He belly-laughed. "You're so funny! I love *The Beverly Hillbillies*!"

I was about to ask Giorgio about Dr. Hotz's plan to treat him, when track manager Joe Messina nosed in. His gold tooth glinted.

"Tony the Tiger, I hear you're going to race with Giorgio. Can't wait to watch you two tearing it up!" His voice was phlegmy and cracked from years of smoking and yelling over the roar of 900 horse-power engines.

I was immediately suspicious of him. This seemed to be my default setting these days. Cynical and angry.

'Tony the Tiger' had been my first racetrack nickname, back when I was a kid. Hearing it now made my heart ache. My old track family had been so good to me. I'd grown up around people like Joe.

"Yeah, well, whatever it takes to help Giorgio win," I finally said, "although I'm a total rust bucket, so probably no help at all." I turned to Giorgio.

Joe rubbed his hands together. "If you guys need anything, anything at all, just let me know. Okay?"

He raised an eyebrow at Randy, who was holding a dead-straight headstand for as long as possible, just in case the Guinness World Records happened to show up, I guess. Joe shrugged and headed down the laneway.

He met up with the first responders, who seemed glad to see him. Maybe he really was a good guy, but I couldn't afford to trust so easily. For all I knew, he was just another mob greaseball, manipulating me with fake decency.

"Really, really great guy," Giorgio said, dreamily. "Eh? That Joe."

Who the hell was he talking about? Tom Hanks? "Oh yeah, helluva guy." I leaned on the sprint car, trying not to look cynical.

"C'mon, Tony, give it a spin!"

What choice did I have?

I climbed into the white and red car. It fit my body like a glove, of course. I tried not to moan out loud.

Like a doting parent, Giorgio leaned his head through the open window. "Take your time, OK? Safety first. I mean it. If something ever happened to you, I couldn't live with myself." For a split second, his face crumpled, as if he was about to bawl. The kid really was anxious for me. It did something funny to my gut.

Other than Angie and Ma and Josie and Norb, no other adult had shown their concern for me the way Giorgio had. I felt like I'd just witnessed the kid's open-heart surgery.

"Hey Giorgio," I called after him, as he jogged to his car. "After we're done, we'll do a debrief, and I'll give you some tips."

If this project with Giorgio went well, maybe I could be a racing instructor. Angel was getting older, so now I didn't have to be home every single night. But instead of being excited by the idea of coaching, for some reason I found it depressing.

Giorgio looked back at me. "Tony," he said bashfully, "I'm sure you have great tips, but I'm already a really good driver. Honest." He kicked the dirt. "I just need help with my anxiety so I don't keep losing all the time."

Well, maybe he was a really good driver. I'd soon find out. But he definitely had insecurities. "Keep seeing Dr. Hotz."

"Oh, I will," he said. "She's super keen!"

I just nodded, trying to look enthused.

Energized, he got his helmet out of the car. But before he pulled it on, he tucked earpieces into his ears.

"What's with the ear pieces?" I asked.

"Oh yeah, I forgot to tell you. Dr. Hotz is coaching me through the turns." He pointed excitedly up at the stands.

Sitting there, wearing a headset with a microphone, was Dr. Hotz. She waved at us and then went serious-looking, in "therapy mode", as she called it.

Interesting.

Like an over-excited kid thrilled to finally be getting on the roller coaster after a long wait in line, he jumped into Goldilocks awkwardly, knocking his helmet against the frame. But then he quickly shook it off, re-adjusted his helmet and gave me a final thumbs up.

That's when it dawned on me—Giorgio was ten times the people pleaser Norb was. He had a desperate need to make everyone happy, make everyone proud of him. It was a hell of a jail cell to put yourself in. Putting everyone else's needs ahead of your own well-being? Okay in small doses. As a life strategy, however, it sucked. Maybe I could help him win, but for himself. Not to make anyone else happy. Just for Giorgio.

Randy toppled out of his headstand and rolled to his feet in front of my car. He double-tapped his pinky against his temple, popped the hood, then laid hands on the engine. "Chi injection. Godspeed. Tony goes to heaven," he chanted, like a Buddhist monk or something.

"Cut the bullshit, Randy!"

Swaying gently, he was acting like he was channeling some kinda cosmic energy. Maybe he was. Who the frig knew anymore?

But I couldn't be mad at him now. I'd developed a soft spot for him, the way I had for my pal Donny. But I'd sure as hell never tell Randy that. I wasn't Mother friggin' Theresa.

He shut the hood and skittered away, pleased with his woo-woo moment, I guess.

Tanner showed up in a red Chevy pick-up and push-started Giorgio, while Joe pushed me with Randy's truck.

I pushed the gear handle down.

This was really happening!

With trembling hands, I flipped the fuel switch. Joe pushed faster. The needle in the pressure gauge rose. The rear wheels turned over. Oil pressure built up. I flipped the Mag switch.

The engine roared to life and I hit the gas! The thrust yanked me back against the seat.

My body felt electric, my heart a thundering bass drum.

Sweet Jesus, Mary, and Joseph! It felt amazing!

I whooped like a teenager.

The car throttled nice and stinkin' loud. I flew around Giorgio. I hadn't planned to show off, but my competitive instincts had taken over.

I faltered a little in the first few turns, still struggling with the valve handle that controlled the wing—it was stiff. But by about the fifth lap, I'd gotten used to it and ran the turns *tight*.

Giorgio would sometimes pull up beside me and wave enthusiastically, like a little kid in a bumper car.

I was laughing, from deep down in my belly. I realized how pent-up I'd been lately. If I'd creamed my jeans right then, I probably wouldn't have cared.

When we hit the sixth lap, Giorgio roared up beside me and saluted. But this time, instead of falling back to give me space, he gunned it past me, leaving me to eat his dust.

"Fuck you, Giorgio!" I shouted playfully.

It was on. And the Prodigy wasn't backing down.

By the end of lap twenty, we ran neck-and-neck, sliding through the final turn like something choreographed. When we hit the straightaway, he signalled me to slow down and head to the pit.

When I stopped, I was so pumped I actually leapt out of my car. You'd think *I'd* won the Special!

"You were awesome!" he cried, running over. "No wonder they call you the Prodigy!" He pulled me into a bear hug.

"Like riding a bike," I gasped. I ignored the thoughts that were hammering in my brain—that I shouldn't have quit racing, that I'd had the right friggin' stuff. "You were great, too, Giorgio. You hit those curves like a champ." I clapped him on the back.

"Thanks to Dr. Hotz. The stuff she said to me in my headset really helped."

Dr. Hotz, miracle-worker.

We were interrupted by raucous cheering. Beppe, Uncle Toto, Doughboy, Dad, Joe, and Tanner were looking pretty damn elated. Resentment soured my joy.

Joe hustled down to greet me. "You were awesome, Tony! You're still the Prodigy. So good to have you back."

A wall slid down inside me. "No, *Giorgio* was great. And no, I'm not back. After Giorgio wins, I'm gone. End of story."

Down the way, my responder fans cranked up a Guns N' Roses tune. They shot me the devil horns and rocked out to "Welcome to the Jungle."

I gave them a thumbs-up, which slid smoothly into a middle finger for Dad. But he was too busy chatting up his mobster cronies to notice. *You better not be telling everyone how proud you are of me*, I thought. *Don't you dare be proud of me!*

Focussing on Giorgio's smile helped me ignore the fucktards in the stands. "So, how exactly did the good doctor help you?"

"She whispered all these helpful mindfulness techniques into my ear," he swooned. "And for the first time ever, my hand felt loose and

relaxed on the wing lever. I normally grip it so hard my hand aches."
He suddenly paled. "But what if that was a one-time thing? What if I
freeze up again in a real race? What then, Tony The Tiger?"

"Don't worry about it," I said. "Dr. Hotz will have you sorted out
by race day."

"Goody, goody, gumdrops!" he said, clapping.

Okay, I was starting to love the kid, but this chirpy, *Leave It To
Beaver* stuff was getting on my nerves. I rallied to keep my annoyance
under wraps.

"So, a couple of notes for you," I said. "Your car. Torsion's off. And
the suspension's loose. So are the shocks. You were bouncing out there
like a Super Ball." I *knew* I'd checked all these things after re-assembling
the engine. Had Randy set up the problems to see if I'd notice? Fucking
guy had a lot of nerve, surprise-quizzing me like I was his Grade Nine
auto class student.

Giorgio was chewing on his nubbed-out fingernails. "I'm sorry,
Tony. Was it me? Did I do something wrong?"

"No, no! Don't sweat it, buddy. Nothing to do with you. Randy
and I will wrench it right. When we're done, you'll feel like you're
driving a new car, a *faster* car."

But I could tell he wasn't convinced.

"I promise, okay?"

He sighed. "Okay, Prodigy." But he kept gnawing at his nails.

Randy popped up beside me, humming "Georgia". I felt my anger
kick in.

"Did you fuck with the car after all the work you had me do on it?
Huh?" I leaned toward him, wanting to wipe the smug, crazy smile off
his face.

"Good work, Tiger. You caught the play." He chucked me under
the chin, putting his life in jeopardy.

Suddenly, Randy dropped to his knees, searching for something he'd dropped. He was in a panic, his high-pitched whine getting louder the longer he scrambled.

Giorgio leaned over him. "Need help, Randy?"

Randy suddenly relaxed. "Nope. Got it. Lucky nickel." He squirreled it back in his pocket and stood, looking for all the world like that pathetic little moment had never happened.

I had a powerful craving for mint chip chocolate ice cream, my go-to stress treat. My desire to thump Randy Rocket had drained away.

"Getting late, boys," Joe Messina said, approaching, clapping his hands. "Time to wrap it up."

I checked my watch. "Eleven o'clock. Shit!"

Randy wagged his finger at me. "Family man. Fuck-up. Late. Kid disappointed. Bad Dad."

Nope. My urge to whack him had not disappeared, after all.

Dialed-out, he skipped off towards the clubhouse.

"At least I *am* a family man, Randy! Not a deadbeat dad like *you!*" Yelling after him was juvenile, but I couldn't help it.

"Ouch," Giorgio said. "C'mon now, Tiger. It's just Randy."

Guilt stabbed my chest. "Okay, sorry, I shouldn't have said that. The guy can't help it. He's not right in the head."

In fact, Randy was both nuts *and* tragic. I felt sorry for the guy. Did he deserve it? I mean, the guy had several ex-wives and kids, and he *was* a deadbeat dad. But how much of that had to do with him being a prick versus being mental? Which came first, the chicken or the egg?

My moment of being Mister Compassionate came to an abrupt end. Beside the jabbering mobsters in the stands, Dad turned and fake-smiled me, at least that's how I saw it. The gall! *He* was the reason I wasn't home! The reason my family life was in the shitter!

Fuck you, Father.

As I stumped towards the clubhouse, Beppe and his crew made their way to the edge of the stands, so they could look down on me. I felt like a cow in a slaughterhouse chute.

"You're gonna help my Giorgio win!" Beppe shouted, stabbing the air with his stogie. "I just know it!"

"Fuck off," I grumped.

Beppe threw his arms out dramatically. "Though this be madness, yet there is method in't." He kept yammering away.

Madness? You bet. Who was he quoting? Shakespeare? Margaret Fucking Atwood? Who knew? I'd spent most of my English classes reading *Hot Rod* magazine under my desk. His Eminence's brilliance was lost on me.

But Beppe's toadies applauded. He made an elegant bow. *Buncha weirdos. Easy for you pricks to have a laugh at my expense. You're not the ones stuck trying to achieve the impossible!*

I was almost at the clubhouse door when I went numb and had to stop. Tears welled up in my eyes. My hands were shaking. I was struck with the realization that racing with Giorgio had made me really, really happy, a feeling I hadn't had in years, if I was being honest with myself.

And—fuck it—once this assignment was over, I'd never get to do this again. I was going to have to quit. And deal with the heartbreak again. Dammit!

Inside the van I turned up "Desperado" by Alice Cooper. When I launched the van out of the parking lot past the clubhouse, I caught a glimpse of something out of the corner of my eye. A shadow.

Filming me!

Chapter 13

WEDNESDAY, SEPTEMBER 7, 7:30 p.m.

Tim Horton's at Flux Road and Molson Boulevard.

"Now that I know Walker is a super villain," Norb was saying. "I have to see reality differently now. Sheesh."

He sipped his 3X3 coffee—he was still laying off the 4X4's in an effort to lose some beef. But instead, the poor bastard had packed on more. Stress from losing his mother, fighting The Screw, and fatherhood, I figured.

"You don't have to change the way you see reality, Norb," I said, patting his back. "You know Walker really isn't a super villain, right? He's just a man."

"I guess," Norb said doubtfully.

"Well," I said, half-jokingly. "It's not like he parted the Red Sea." I couldn't remember anything from high school English, but I did remember a thing or two from Sunday school. Maybe because Mrs. Pizzarelli used to give us home-made cannoli whenever we remembered our verses.

"I wish I could part the Red Sea," Norb said, wistfully, "then I'd be like Aquaman. Hans would love that."

Honestly, sometimes it was like talking to an eight-year-old. Besides, I didn't think a toddler would care, not even Norb's son.

"Where the hell's Donny?" I asked, more snappy than necessary.

John and Norb just shrugged.

Then John nailed me with a knowing look. "Spill, Tony-O. What's going on in that head of yours? I can see the wheels turning." He whispered. "You aren't planning to *murder* Walker, are you?" He grinned. Hilarious.

Norb gawped at me, horrified.

"Oh, for eff's sake, Norb you know I wouldn't do that!" I scowled at him. "Even though I'd like to!"

Norb slowly shook his head.

I stared out the window at the Canadian Tire garage on the other side of the parking lot.

Working days there and then doing nights at the track was burning me out. Yesterday, I'd fallen asleep on the creeper during an oil change. I woke up covered in Pennzoil synthetic, and I wasn't going to live that one down, ever. And every time I went to the track, I couldn't shake the terrible fear that Randy had torn apart Giorgio's engine again. I was so tired, I wasn't sure I'd be able to re-assemble it.

But, most of all, I was stressed knowing how seriously re-addicted I'd become to racing. Once this nightmare was over, I'd have to go through withdrawal like a heroin addict fresh off the needle.

Desperate, I'd called this meeting. Third time ever. Hopefully the last. But over the past three weeks, Walker had invaded my privacy—all of ours, in fact—and now it was time we dealt with the prick.

It went against the grain not to deal with this shit on my own, but I was time-crunched and needed my buddies to help me.

"Don't do anything rash!" Angie had cried from the doorway as I'd stormed out of the house. She knew how I felt about Walker, and she'd been furious at him, too, but she worried that I'd do more than just talk about it. She wasn't wrong. A real man would do anything to protect his family.

John's pointy shoe was bouncing up and down. I hoped he'd ram it up Walker's ass when we caught him. *If we caught him.* Donny and Norb had been right when they'd said Walker was a rubber man. Of course, he was also a harassing, piece-of-shit!

My pulse was pounding again. I took a deep breath to calm myself.

The door swung open and in walked an odd-looking dude. I'd seen plenty of oddballs in Hamilton but this guy was more off than your usual cook. He was followed by three buddies.

It was Wednesday, Donny's Incognito Night! Shit! Why couldn't they have gone to McDonalds, instead?

They were a real bunch of winners, let me tell you. First there was a guy dressed up as Humpty-fucking-Dumpty, Norb's alter-ego, created by none other than our pal and lifelong attention whore, Donny Love. He'd barely been able to squeeze through the doorway in his enormous egg costume, his legs ridiculous in red tights.

Then there was a fool costumed as Ace Ventura, Pet Detective. I couldn't stand this Incognito shit, but Patricia *had* done a great job swishing the guy's hair like Jim Carrey's

Arm-in-arm with him was Dolly Parton, in a tight white pant suit studded with sparkly rhinestones. Her wig was a puff of white angel hair. The males in the coffee shop were laser-focussed on her massive breasts, even though they were obviously not real.

But who was the fourth idiot?

Donny Love, of course. He brought his coffee and donut over to our table, while Dolly and Jim and Humpty headed for an open table beside us.

John ripped the words right out of my mouth. "You dressed up as *Dave Walker*, Donny? The prick who's been stalking and harassing us? You're sick, man!"

Donny had nailed it: beige shirt and running shoes, khaki pants, a yellow t-shirt, puffy brown hair, side-parted and swooped across his forehead. Only in Grade 12 did Walker start wearing jeans and Rush t-shirts.

"No," Norb whispered in horror.

"I'm perfectly fine, John," Donny said, unexplainably speaking with some kind of English accent and sounding like Mick Jagger. "Just out for a night of fun, that's all."

"Bullshit!" I growled. "Walker isn't English! And the guy was basically a mute! So there's no way you have any idea how he talks!"

The coffee shop ground down to a screeching halt.

Humpty, who'd really struggled to sit his massive egg-ass on a chair, shushed us with white-gloved hands. "Now, settle down everyone." His voice was sticky sweet.

What the eff? The Captain of the Freak Team didn't want a scene? Norb just gave him nervous side-eye glances. The Humpty Dumpty media fiasco (again, courtesy of *Donny*) was still a trigger for him.

"I'm with you darlin'," Dolly agreed, her missile-sized breasts glittering under the pot-lights.

"Well, alllllll-righty then!" Ace Ventura cried, his face like stretched taffy. Pockets of laughter exploded around us. Residents of The Hammer were nothing, if not pragmatic. If they couldn't get these weirdos out of their coffee shop, then they'd just get on with their caffeine fix and accept the situation.

Humpty stood up, awkwardly knocking over his chair with a clatter, and bowed. "Carry on, good people of Hamilton!"

"Wow," Norb said, suddenly thrilled with the theatrics. "This is so awesome!"

But John looked pissed off, like me.

My anger with Donny finally boiled over. He should have known better than to show up like this, in his silly Incognito costume. He knew how important this meeting was to me, to all of us. And why had he brought his nutty friends?

In fury, I air-punched in the general direction of his face.

Donny's eyes went wide. "Woah, Tony! Relax!"

"He doesn't normally act like this," Norb apologized to Dolly. She smiled uneasily.

"Knock it off, Tony," John grumbled.

But now I was punching the air faster, imagining Donny's face was a speed bag.

Ace Ventura leapt up, grinning like a maniac. "Let's get back to those donuts, shall we? Chop-chop, Captain Violent!"

That got a big laugh from the patrons. But Donny and I were up on our feet now, and my friend's face was scared. Years of his bullshit had finally sent me over the edge! I was *this* close to knocking his block off!

John grabbed my arm to pull me back but I was superhuman with rage.

The three remaining looney toons collectively grabbed the other arm. I held on as long as I could, then finally gassed out, emotionally and physically. I flopped down in my seat, my heart an over-revved engine.

"Sorry," I muttered to everyone, disgusted with myself. I blew my nose into a napkin. Eventually, everyone else sat down again.

After I'd gathered myself, I gave Donny a calm, hard look. "Ditch the costume."

"What's really going on here?" he asked, hesitantly. "You hate my Incognito stuff, I know, but what's eating you, really?"

The fucker could read me, like he had some kind of supernatural radar.

I glared at the dopes beside us. "Do you mind? Private Conversation."

Dolly and Humpty politely looked away, but Ace just smirked at me. I sighed.

"I need your help, man," my voice cracking as I looked at my friend. "All of your help. 'Cause with everything else that's going on, this Walker bullshit is gonna make me lose my mind. If you can't help me, I honest to God don't know..." My cheeks burned with embarrassment. I was supposed to be self-reliant and tough. I shoved on my bulldog face, my armour.

Even though they supposedly weren't eavesdropping on us, Dolly daubed at her eyes with a tissue and Humpty sniffed a couple times. Ace just scratched his ass.

Donny beamed. "Straight up I'll help you, Tone. What's up? What's going on?" He tore off his wig and leaned across the table, jazzed.

The words hammered out of me. "Look, everywhere I go, Walker's filming me. The track, the mall, Village Variety, out for a walk, you name it. But whenever I chase him, he's already gone. Like a frickin' ghost or a ninja or something! Why's he filming me? Why? Maybe there's no film in his camera. Maybe it's just an evil tactic to drive us all insane."

You could hear a pin drop, except for the distant chatter at the take-out window.

"Today, I was out on my lunch break, shooting the shit with the sausage man when I saw Walker filming me through his car window. I whipped my sausage at him but, as usual, he'd already caught the play—like he'd set me up to react like that—and was already half-way out the parking lot burning rubber, and *somehow* the fucker even managed to keep filming me while he drove! God dammit!"

"Waste of a perfectly good sausage," Norb empathized.

"And get this," I continued. "He keeps driving up to my house on an old ten-speed bike."

"What?" John snorted.

"Yeah, with his stupid Super 8." I wiped sweat off my brow. "What about my family? What's his game? Is he dangerous? Huh? I don't deserve this. None of us do."

"Maybe it's what you didn't do in high school," Donny said, thoughtfully. "Like say hi to him once in a while."

"Know what else I didn't do? Punch him in the head! Just because you didn't notice a guy in high school doesn't mean you bullied him. If that was true, then *everyone* at Irondale was a bully. Even Norb."

Norb looked offended.

"There, there, darlin'," Dolly said to him. "Why, you sure aren't a bully. You're just as sweet as cherry pie." She reached over and gently poked his nose. It was uncomfortable for everyone but Norb.

"I remember my old Targa ten-speed," Donny said, glad to be changing the subject. "They were *so* cool."

"Naw, they were rattly," John said. "Sekines all the way."

Pissed off by the pathetic attention span of my audience, I snapped my fingers. "He films me opening my mailbox, and when I tear across the lawn to rip him a new one, he zips off on his bike like greased lightning. Is this only happening to me?"

"Last Monday," Norb piped up, "Walker showed up at my shop, pretending to browse. He had on a huge hoodie, so I couldn't see his face, but he looked like half my regulars, so I didn't give it a second thought. I'd forgotten about him until Tank got my attention. Walker had pulled out his camera. I finally recognized him! And the bugger was filming me! When I told him to stop, he laughed like a hyena and zinged out the door!" Norb had full jimmy legs going under the table now.

"Hey, Norb, it's OK, man. Take a breath." I nodded. "Who wouldn't be stressed out?"

"Damn," John said, "he's been filming me, too." He swiped at invisible dust on his shoe. "And he did some other shit that's messed up my head..." John's voice faltered. "I've been doing well, you know. And I just really...want to stay healthy."

"What the fuck did he do, John?" I growled. My fears were grinding gears in my head.

"Language, young man," Humpty chided me.

"I will crack your shell, pal. I swear I will." There was no more commentary from the egg man.

"Tell us John," Norb urged.

John closed his eyes and scowled. "The bastard showed up at my studio for a free salsa lesson!"

"A...free salsa lesson?" Donny was puzzled.

"Was he a bad dancer?" Norb offered helpfully.

"Are you sure it was him?" Donny added.

"Not at first. It was like he had this charisma you had to wade through first. He was stroking his chin, like a professor deep into a philosophy lecture. And he had on this huge signet ring. He swirled his hands around, and the ring had this sort-of hypnotic glint." He swallowed. "And he was quick on his feet, a natural. After about five minutes, he'd aced all the beginner moves. No one does that. Not unless they're already trained."

"He was a spellcaster," Norb said. "Like a wizard."

"Then what?" I was impatient to figure out the creepy mystery of Dave Walker, Wizard and Loony Toon.

"On Monday, half-way through the advanced class, he showed in the doorway, filming everyone."

"Of course he was," Donny said in a grim voice.

John's face had gone white.

"John," Donny said, nervously. "Are you okay, man?"

"Being filmed wasn't the sick part," he stammered. "Not even close."

"Sick part?" Donny said. "How much crazier does this guy get?"

John faced Donny. "Walker was *you*, Donny. Make-up, clothing, the works. He even grinned your stupid grin. He was fucking spot-on!" He looked completely spooked.

Norb wasn't the only person who gasped. Dolly's wig quivered with her indignation, and Ace Ventura's eyebrows took turns jumping up to his hairline.

"Walker impersonated *me*?" Donny's eyes narrowed. *"Me?"*

It occurred to a little, tiny, unworthy part of me that this was hilariously ironic. Karma, if you will. Donny was getting a taste of his own medicine.

"I'm afraid so," John said. "He obviously wanted me to see him impersonating you."

"Then what did he do?" Norb asked.

"What he always does. Took off. If I hadn't had a class to finish, I would have chased after him."

Donny laughed hard, once, like a bark. Thoughts jittered behind his eyes. Grim-faced, he hit speed-dial on his phone.

How much worse could things get? I suddenly wished I could escape in a hot air balloon like John had. I wanted to fuck off to a magic land, far away from Beppe, the mob, my dad and his debt, and psycho Walker.

Donny was talking to someone now. "He said we're old *friends*?...I don't care that he offered you twice our usual rate. What happened to your code of ethics, huh? I seriously doubt he's funnier than me!" Donny's face went fire-engine red. "Did he say why?...Yes, Patricia, I understand you're a professional and you don't ask questions, but I'm pretty sure Walker's a seriously deranged psycho, and you shouldn't have been alone with him. *I'll* pay you twice as much to never put him in make-up again!...I never asked to be impersonated!" He hung up and glared at the table.

I had no clue how Dave Walker had gotten a hold of Patricia. Maybe he'd overheard a conversation? Or maybe he'd been stalking Donny, too.

"Donny," Norb peeped. "You and your friends impersonate people all the time without asking permission. So why are you so upset Walker's doing the same thing?"

Donny raised his glare to Norb, who shrivelled away from him.

"Because he got a taste of his own medicine, and nobody likes that," John said. "Plus, Walker is apparently just as good at disguising himself as the Maestro here, so Donny's jealous."

"That's enough John," I said. Yes, John had hit the nail on the head, but it was still kind of a mean remark.

But Donny wasn't letting John off the hook. "How dare you, Dr. Fucking Freud," he blubbered. "I would never be jealous of that rubbery, scheming, maniac!"

He grabbed a napkin and smudged off his Walker make-up, which was kind of ironic. You know, the two wackadoos impersonating each other. Donny must've realized that, because his face went red.

"OK, I guess you're right, John," he said quietly. "About everything." He snorted. "It's time I saw Walker for who he really is—a fucking loser with a camera."

Norb was busy daubing his tears. He really hated it when there was conflict between any of us guys. He looked pleadingly at John and me.

John blew out a sigh. "Look, I'm sorry I said all that, Donny. I'm not a psychologist. I had no right to analyze you like that. Especially not in public." He gave an evil eye to the looky-loos around the coffee shop. "Can I get you a fresh coffee, buddy?"

But Donny didn't answer him. He sagged in his chair, exhausted and dejected. John went and got him one, anyway.

I had a strong feeling that tonight's news might bring about some growth in Donny Love, like married and raising kids had been for me and Norb, or marriage had been for John. Despite his own marriage and fatherhood, Donny hadn't changed in any consistent way. He was still up and down and all over the map, most of the time. It had to be exhausting living like that. I crossed my fingers for the poor bastard.

Then I remembered Walker had been in a local punk band, Little Boxes, back in the day. They'd had about fifteen minutes of fame, but still. Maybe for Donny it was like his obsession with Steven Dundee. Donny always longed for *more*. More attention, more love, more talent, more fame.

"Donny," I asked, "did Walker's band ever make it big?"

"No. And I'm glad they didn't. Walker's become an artist in his own right. A really great jazz guitarist, actually. It's good he never went big."

"So, you don't care that he's not famous?" Norb asked.

"Nope, Norb, I don't. That's not important. It's about the art. It's all in the doing. The rest is bullshit and it always was. I was just too blind to see it."

I picked my jaw up off the table.

John had just returned with Donny's coffee. He gave me a doubtful look. "So you've *heard* Walker play?" he asked Donny.

"Oh yeah. At first, I thought I was listening to Wes Montgomery, you know, that song "Four On Six", but then I heard Walker's amp feedback. He'd nailed it note-for-note. Just incredible."

I had a bad feeling. "Where exactly did you hear him?"

"Outside his house," he said, uneasily.

Donny was pathetic. But for once I couldn't get mad at him.

"I was half-way up his front steps when I heard his music. I was curious so I followed it around to the side of his house and stopped under his bedroom window. But I kinda wished I hadn't."

"Why?" Norb was on the edge of his seat.

Donny looked away. "Hearing him play was...soul-destroying. He's just so talented. I'd wasted my life, practicing my mediocre ass for nothing." Remorse drained his colour. "So, yeah, I'm a stalker and a Peeping Tom."

Norb patted his back. "Hey, you're too hard on yourself. You're a fine guitarist, too. Seriously!"

"Damn right," I said. "You rock AC/DC like no one's business."

"And American Woman. And you've almost nailed the Stairway to Heaven solo," John added.

"Thanks, guys," Donny sighed.

"But no more lurking under bedroom windows," John warned. "If Walker has security cameras you'll be on tape and the cops *will* charge you." He lowered his head. "I ought to know. I still can't believe I stalked Sophia. I'm lucky I didn't end up in jail." He looked pretty ashamed.

I watched Donny carefully. I knew that he probably wouldn't stop stalking Walker until he'd seen him face-to-face and grilled him with a thousand personal, prying questions. Donny's obsessions rarely went on vacation.

And if it was true that I was mad at Donny for his Walker drama (and I was), the way I'd often been with John's Sophia drama and Norb's Screw drama, then it was also true I was mad at myself for my own Daddy drama. I was just as messed up as my friends! How was that possible? I was supposed to be the sensible one, the guy with two feet firmly on the ground!

Right then, Donny leapt up as if he'd seen a ghost, pointing an accusatory finger. Everyone turned to look.

"Not again!" Donny cried. "You're stalking me! You talented, fucking prick!"

A hush descended.

"Cussin' sweetheart," Dolly warned under her breath.

Walker was three tables over, wearing a black hoodie and mirrored sunglasses, filming us.

"You nervy fucking bastard!" I thundered, jumping and knocking my chair over. I was going to punch out that a-hole's lights!

Before I'd gone two steps, Walker was rubbering out the door.

We all barreled out after him.

Walker dove feet first into his car and roared it towards Flux Road. Donny managed to jump on the hood, but slid off the far side onto the pavement. It was like something out of an action movie.

"Donny, are you okay?" John cried, racing towards him.

Donny sat up abruptly, swaying a little. How banged up was he?

Donny's Incognito pals came running toward him, looking even more ludicrous out there in the parking lot.

Donny sprang to his feet, enraged. "Come back here you fucking coward!"

Already out on Molson Boulevard, Walker beeped his horn in triumph.

Humpty chased after Donny on his tippy-toes, surprisingly fast.

When he caught up to Donny, he pulled him into a bear hug. Donny began to sob like a little boy. I didn't know which way to look. The poor fool had finally overloaded.

But this wasn't the first time I'd seen one of my friends this upset. I remembered Norb at his mom's funeral, crying in a voice I didn't recognize. I wasn't good with that stuff.

I hated crying. I did my best to avoid it. And crying in front of someone else? No effing way!

Donny's crying discovered a new gear. It became infectious. Virtually everyone within earshot was teary. A guy on his scooter was bawling so hard he almost fell off.

Humpty finally released Donny and Dolly passed out tissues. Tears were mopped up and noses blown. Ace Ventura just dragged this sleeve across his nose and declared the whole situation a "bummer".

Awkwardly, I squeezed Donny's shoulder. "We're here for you, buddy. Always. You ever need anything, you let me know, okay?"

"Thanks," he snuffled.

This whole bizarre impersonation thing had messed him right up. His nerves were obviously shot, but I'd been so caught up in my own mess that I'd failed to see the state he was in.

Moving forward, I vowed to myself that I'd be nicer to Donny, and everyone else, the way John had tried since marrying Sheena. I needed to remember that people might be dealing with crap that I didn't see. And even though Donny could push my buttons more than anyone else I knew, he deserved some TLC. Hell, we all did.

"Hang in there, Love," John said. "We'll deal with Walker later." He clapped Donny's back.

"Damn right we will," he said, his voice shaking, but he sounded doubtful. His ears burned red with embarrassment and there was a bloody cut on his cheek.

"Thanks, everyone, but I need to be alone now."

The crowd drifted off. The three Incognito weirdos said their goodbyes and piled into a van straight out of Scooby-Doo.

"Do you want me to take you to the hospital?" I asked, taking a closer look at that cut.

"Nah, I'm fine. Just a little bruised up."

"You were really brave," Norb said. "That was an epic move. Mission Impossible epic."

John had a grim look on his face. "Stalkers always come back, and when he does, *we'll* stalk *him*."

I was careful not to tease John about being an expert on stalking.

Donny rode home with me, but he didn't say a word the whole way. I was worried about him. He hadn't been that quiet since the time he'd missed scoring on an open net during road hockey finals. The Machine Shop Psychos won the cup that year. Donny'd been so down on himself he wouldn't answer our calls or come to his door for a month.

As I pulled into his driveway, he was so pale and withdrawn I barely recognized him.

"You gonna be okay, Love?"

He shrugged.

"You'll bounce back, buddy," I said playfully, trying to cheer him up. "It's what you do."

No response, so I tried again. "Don't let me down, *Rubber Man*!"

He slugged out of my van into the darkness of his porch. The light from inside his house spilled through the door as he walked in. He didn't turn back to wave.

All the way home, I brooded.

Chapter 14

What was supposed to be a stress-free night didn't last long. As soon as Angel had flown down the basement stairs, a knot had started to ache in my neck and my chest had tightened.

She'd hounded me to buy new slot cars, the sprint car versions. Guilty over my recent absences, I bought her some from Clive's Hobby Shop on Concession Street. Mine was number 9, red, a Goodyear sticker on its wing. Angel's was purple, her latest favourite colour, with several newly-added sparkly unicorn stickers on the doors.

She'd thrown on her blue racing suit and was skillfully triggering her controller and whipping her car around the track. She chomped on gum, blowing bubbles so loud it was like the cracking of a whip.

Then I realized what was really bugging me. When she saw me glaring at her, she made a tough-guy face, just the image of her old dad, and not in a good way.

Angie was perched on a barstool with a beer. She smirked at me. This new version of our daughter, cocky and wilful, had been giving her mom trouble lately, and now apparently it was my turn.

I threw her a desperate look, but she'd already turned back to her magazine.

I faced our ten-year old. "You're kidding, right?"

"Dad!" She crossed her arms hard against her chest. The way I did when I was mad.

"Take it off," I snapped. "You're too young for make-up. You look like a—" I stopped myself, instantly regretting what I'd almost said. *What's wrong with you, man! She's just a kid!*

"Tony," Angie said sharply.

Had I missed this sudden change in my kid because I'd been stuck at the track and was hardly ever home? I felt panicky, blindsided. Angel had always been my little racer girl. Her and me all the way. I'd always thought she'd be safe from boys until much later.

"Like a what, Dad?" Angel angrily pumped her controller and burned rubber down the straight-away, leaving my car in the dust.

I tried not to be hurt that recently she'd stopped calling me "Daddy". "Like someone I don't recognize," I said, relieved to have found something better to say than *slut*. "Honey, you're ten, okay, not sixteen. So, please, go upstairs and take off that make-up and let's just play slot cars and have fun like we always do."

"Dad! All the girls wear make-up! It's only mascara and lip gloss. It's not like I'm wearing fake nails and foundation."

"You don't need to be like other girls, Angel. You're a Kart racer. You don't need make-up. And you think for yourself. Besides, I don't want you growing up so fast. It's not how you think it is." I looked to Angie for support but she was ignoring me, leafing through a *Hot Rod* magazine she had absolutely no interest in.

Our daughter was growling like a tomcat. Only time I'd heard her that mad was when Frankie used to tease her. She'd come out swinging her fists, which he easily blocked, pissing her off even more.

My helpful wife just swigged some beer and gave me a brief sympathetic look. I was on my own.

In my shock, I'd let my car slow, so I put the pedal to the metal in an effort to catch up. She had me by three laps. Even the Prodigy couldn't catch her now. I hoped her sense of competition would distract her from her bad mood.

Why had my kid chosen today of all days to wear make-up? I'd really been looking forward to stress-free father-daughter time. Suddenly, hanging out with Randy and Giorgio at the track seemed way less stressful than dealing with all this.

Last time at the track, I'd found myself thinking *no wonder Dad was never home—hanging out here is awesome!* And then I'd immediately felt completely disgusted with myself. I reminded myself that after Giorgio raced, win or lose, I was gone for good and back to being a good family man. End of story.

Unfortunately, the silence between my daughter and me had grown heavier than a Ford Big Block engine. It hurt so much I could barely stand it. I'd never in a million years have taken her for a girly-girl. And at age ten? Seriously? What next? High heels and mini-skirts? And was she about to tell me she was quitting racing?

"I hope you're not trying to get a boyfriend?" I blurted against my better judgement.

She looked horrified. "Dad!"

"Tony," Angie said, finally jumping in. "A lot of girls her age experiment with a little make-up. It's not a big deal. It's normal. You're over-reacting."

"Fine, fine, forget I said anything," I grumbled. "Sorry. Obviously, I suck at this stuff. Let's just race."

Angel stopped her car. "Dad?" Her eyes were full of tears. She'd gone from mad to sad in a heartbeat. "Do you hate Nonno?" She looked terrified to hear the answer, but determined too.

I froze up.

Okay, so she was being direct with me about Dad. Confrontational. I hadn't raised her to be a coward, so I wasn't surprised. And this was way better than make-up.

"Well, honey, that's complicated. Like I always say, when you're eighteen, I'll tell you the whole story. I promise."

She crossed her arms again and began tapping her racing shoe. She wasn't letting me off the hook, not this time. "Once I heard Frankie tell Viviana that when you were a kid Nonno was a gangster and he was never home and that's why you hate him. Is that true?"

I felt as if I was looking at two Angels, one pissed off and wearing make-up, and the other Daddy's little chip-off-the-block racing girl who was five again and desperately needed her daddy's reassurance.

"Lose the make-up and maybe I'll tell you." As soon as I heard myself say it, I knew I was just swinging wildly at the ball now. Shit. Why was parenting so hard?

She slapped her hand against the table and stomped up the stairs.

Half-way up, she spun around. "If Giorgio loses, will Nonno and Nonna live with us?" Her lower lip was trembling.

Shitshitshit. "Uh, I haven't thought that far ahead, honey. And he's not going to lose. So you don't need to worry about it."

"You should be nicer to Nonno!" she cried. "He's nice to you but you always treat him like shit!"

"Watch your language!" I roared.

She ran up the stairs, sobbing and raging, stomped down the hallway, then slammed her bedroom door. The sound stung my heart. She'd never done that before, but then I'd never yelled at her like that. I'd gone too far. I'd over-reacted. I couldn't remember ever having a scene with our three older kids. My heart burned with regret.

Angie was exasperated with me. Well, what did she expect? She'd left me to deal with it on my own, like a bull in a china shop. She dropped the magazine on the bar and headed for the stairs to go check on our daughter. If that angry tween even *was* our daughter. It seemed more likely she'd been replaced with some kind of alien.

"What the frig's up with her?"

"Welcome to my world," Angie said over her shoulder. She stopped on the top step, ducked her head down and whispered.

"Angelina's ten. In case you haven't noticed, she's becoming a little woman."

"At ten? Ten is still a kid."

"Not so much. Kids grow up faster these days. Some of the girls in Angelina's class have even had their period."

My heart just about stopped. "Seriously?" Menstruation changed *everything*.

"I had mine when I was eleven."

"You did?" How had I not known that?

"It's the hormones in the chicken," I blurted, desperate. "Free range from now on. Or whatever they call it." I only half-believed myself.

"It's not the *chicken*, Tony," she snapped. "It's life. And you're going to have to accept it."

At least she didn't slam the door like Angel had.

I cracked open a beer and took a hard swallow.

Sadness burned in my gut like a hot ingot. My little girl was growing up! For a moment there, she'd looked at me with cold, critical eyes. Had she lost respect for me? Was I no longer her hero?

But she swore! I thought, trying to justify my behaviour. If I'd done that at her age, Dad would have cuffed me. All kids know that you never let your folks hear you cuss. It's a basic rule. Of course, I swore all the time, but never in front of my kids, at least not on purpose.

I took a long, hard swig. Oh God, would she even let me call her "Angel" anymore?

All my kids had gone to catholic School. They'd had Sunday school and catechism classes and all that stuff. They knew that Jesus wouldn't forgive us if we didn't forgive others. So what kind of example had I just set? What must my daughter think of me? I was a hypocrite. I shouldn't have made such a big deal over a stupid word like "shit". I felt so ashamed of myself.

Man, I really could have used a parenting manual. I wasn't ready for this next stage in my kid's life. In the future, I'd pick up on Angie's cues and just shut my big wop mouth. Hopefully.

Angel, I thought, sighing heavily, *one day you'll realize it's not* me *messing you up. It's Nonno! He's made me a casualty! And because of him, you're suffering. But you're too young to understand that right now.*

Thinking of Dad had me seething. It really was all his fault—all of it!

Then something flashed past the basement window, making me jump.

I charged up the stairs, out the front door, and onto the front lawn, but it was wasted effort.

Walker was already ripping down the street in his blue Datsun. There was a huge rust hole in the passenger door. The muffler sounded like a fart machine, adding insult to injury.

I was so paralyzed with fear and anger I couldn't move. My chest heaved up and down, but I couldn't seem to take in oxygen. Walker was an earwig in my brain now, slowly driving me insane. What the fuck was his goal?

At some point, I somehow unstuck myself and paced in circles. I wrapped my arms around myself like a straight-jacket, shaking in the cold night air. Eventually, I stumbled to the porch and sat down.

I considered calling my friends to tell them to come film *me* at Walker's house, kicking the shit out of him, when Angie came outside. The screen door banged behind her as she sat down beside me. The pneumatic closer was shot. I'd been meaning to replace it for months.

"Why'd you run out of the house so fast, hon?"

I didn't want to worry her, so I lied. "I thought I heard footsteps on the front lawn. Thought maybe it was a burglar. Turns out it was just the Elliott boys playing hide-and-seek."

Her expression crinkled. She squeezed my hand, and I realized she was crying. Something was very wrong.

"Is Angel, okay?"

"She's fine. She'll bounce back."

But when I saw the look on her face, I knew my instincts were right. My heart started racing. "Something's fucking wrong, Angie. What is it?"

"Donny called. You need to call him back right away."

"Why?" I asked hesitantly.

"He wouldn't say. But he was really upset. I think something bad has happened, Tony."

I could feel it, like that awful moment before I'd found my childhood dog Bruno dead on the laundry room floor.

Determined to get this over with, I gave my wife a side-hug. We held onto each other as we went back into the house. The kitchen light looked dim to me, and the beige wall phone was the most depressing thing ever invented.

Dread soiled my gut. I wasn't built for life and death shit. Heart thumping, I picked up the phone and dialed.

Chapter 15

Mom had called me and asked me to stop by after work. After what had happened to Archie Love, I was worried she had similar news.

Archie Love had suffered a major heart attack and was in intensive care over at Henderson Hospital. Donny had been so emotional on the phone that I'd gotten choked up, too. I'd offered to visit Archie, but Donny said his dad didn't want anyone *greetin' and girnin'* over him.

To make things worse, apparently Walker had had the cold-hearted nerve to show up in Archie's hospital room, disguised as a janitor. The piece-of-shit was even wearing a body cam!

Donny had chased him down a stairwell and out a fire exit. Hospital security had arrived on the scene too late. Donny was now more determined than ever to nail the prick. And with Donny anything was almost possible.

Ten minutes after I spoke to Donny, Norb called in a panic over an article in *The Hamilton Gazette*. The night was just getting worse. The Screw was seeking early parole!

I figured that Norb had been worried this could happen, because he'd begun training at a new Kung Fu school and had taken to practicing at the gun range with his dad's Luger. Weekends at the Hamilton Gun Club had improved his aim and he was over the moon he'd hit a bullseye. Morag wasn't as thrilled. She made him keep the gun at the range, where the baby couldn't accidently get his hands on it. Norb had informed me that his Steeltown Avenger getup was now hanging in a glass case in the living room, so he could access it quickly when the Screw came a-knockin'.

He'd also had shared some great news. Hans had spoken his first word, calling his dad "Nermy". And not only that, Morag was expecting! Again. I'd ended the call congratulating him and telling him how proud I was of him. It felt awkward as hell, but I knew I was on the right track. I wasn't sure I'd ever get comfortable showing my emotions to my friends, but it was important to do it, anyway.

After those two eventful phone calls, I'd sat with Angie at the kitchen table, voices down.

Angie busted my balls to tell her the real reason why I'd raced out of the house. She had wicked radar for liars. When she graduated from teacher's college, her students would learn pretty fast she didn't take shit from nobody. She knew that I sometimes held back the truth until I was ready to spill, and that some of my truths would never see the light of day, but when it came to truths that affected our family, she'd hound me until I'd told her everything. But that night I just couldn't stress her out with more Walker stories, so I told her I had everything under control and not to worry, that I'd tell her everything after Giorgio's race and then she'd understand. Normally she would have fought me on something like that, but with all my stress, she'd reluctantly given me a pass. I could tell she was struggling really hard this time to be Team Tony.

Then we tackled the topic of our baby girl and her sudden descent into brattiness. Angie delivered the shocking news that her ma had put her on the pill when she was fourteen, afraid she would get pregnant with her boyfriend.

"Mike Anderson?" I'd said, remembering him from Irondale.

"Yep," she said, nodding, "we started early."

"Woah," I said. "I had no idea your Mom was so liberal."

"Not liberal, Tony. Scared out of her mind, more like it. She never told Dad. He would have chased Mike with a cleaver."

"*Please* tell me you're not thinking of putting our little girl on the pill," I said. "She's only ten!" My heart was beginning to race. She could tell I was revving up.

"No, of course not. Calm down, Tone. I just wanted you to know that some girls experiment earlier than others."

"Why didn't you tell me you went on the pill so young? I thought we weren't supposed to keep secrets."

"That wasn't a secret, honey. It happened a long time ago, and I was young. I guess I didn't see a reason to bring it up before." Like I hadn't brought up some of my truths, I thought.

So, I let it go. I was just grateful she hadn't gotten pregnant. Then she would have ended up with Mike, and I would have missed out on the love of my life.

Our other daughters, Viviana and Francesca, hadn't shown any interest in make-up until they were in high school. And neither of them had had serious boyfriends until they'd gone away to university. I prayed our youngest didn't get one until then. Teenage boys could be pigs. Even the nice ones had perverted thoughts. They couldn't help it.

My last mission that night had been to make peace with Angel. When I knocked on her bedroom door, she'd yelled at me to go away. After about ten minutes of knocking and pleading, she said I could come in. She was lying down on her bed, facing the wall, still in her racing suit. A pile of tear-soaked tissues covered the floor. My heart melted for her. I felt so guilty I'd given her a hard time. She looked so young and vulnerable but still she growled, once. So, instead of sitting on her bed, I played safe and just leaned against the door jam. On her vanity table, there was a sparkly pink make-up bag and a comb and brush. Her behavior was normal, I told myself. She was experimenting. It was shitty not to support her during this tough time. Why was it that fathers were the last to understand and accept their daughters' changes? What were we so afraid of? Someone taking advantage of her? Yep. That was it. I sighed. Couldn't she stay young forever? Or at least, a little longer?

"Angel, honey, I'm sorry I gave you a hard time. After listening to your mom, I get it now that it's perfectly normal for girls your age to experiment with make-up. My bad. I'm sorry."

"*Hmpph*," she snuffled, keeping her back to me.

Man, I felt so out of my league here. "I guess I was scared you wouldn't want to be my racing buddy anymore."

"Are you kidding?" she cried, jerking to face me. Her cheeks were wet with tears. "I love racing! I'm going to be a professional when I grow up. You're my hero, Dad. You taught me everything I know. You *are* my racing buddy!"

I'd held on for as long as I could, but the tears finally started to flow, much to my embarrassment. Angel flew from the bed and bear-hugged me. I pressed her against me, filled with relief.

"I love you, Angel."

"I love you, too, Dad."

Now I was driving north on Princeton Drive, then right onto Iron Oak Way. I parked in front of my childhood house, a 1955 reddish brick backsplit with an attached garage. It was proudly Italian-Canadian, with two concrete lions at the end of the drive and enough wrought-iron to build a decent-sized jail.

Dad's car wasn't in the driveway. Obviously, he'd high-tailed it. He knew not to be here alone with Ma and me, that I'd only be around him at Christmas and Thanksgiving, when lots of family were present to act as a buffer. It had been that way for over a decade. That was my deal, take it or leave it.

He'd left the garage door open. The garage was stuffed with old hunting and fishing crap, wine bottles and tomato sauce jars, buckets, and his beloved Toro snowblower and who knew what else. The car had never been parked in the garage, to my knowledge. No room.

I felt a pang of nostalgia for my childhood. I remembered playing road hockey with the neighbourhood kids. Today, more than ever, I wondered what had become of them. Other than fresh paint and modern cars, the neighbourhood hadn't changed all that much. Time had basically frozen it. Old neighbours died, and I sure got older, but the brick houses barely aged.

I let myself in with my key and hollered. "Ma?"

"In the kitchen, Tony."

The house smelled like it always did—tomato sauce, vinegar, bleach, and cigarette smoke. Ma smoked Benson and Hedges. Somehow, she'd made it to sixty-seven without getting lung cancer. Josie joked that what was saving her was the anti-oxidants in her home-made tomato sauce. I hoped.

For decades, we'd begged Ma to stop, but whenever we did she went stone cold silent. Eventually we gave up. It was too stressful.

Because of Ma's second-hand smoke, Dad had a wheeze in his chest. He'd tried for ages to get her to smoke outside but she was stubborn. Maybe it was her way of giving him the middle finger for all the pain he'd caused.

Honestly, though, other than trying to kill herself and her family with cigarettes, my mother was a saint. How she ever ended up with Dad was beyond me. He'd definitely won the lottery—the only lottery that actually mattered.

I kicked off my shoes, bounded up the six steps and crossed the hallway into the kitchen, hoping to find a pan of brownies and a cold glass of milk on the table. No dice.

"Sit, son," she said. "This won't take long."

She drew a smoke from an open pack and lit up, tilting her head to exhale. Smoke circled the old wagon wheel chandelier like a noose.

Ma had a Gina Lollobrigida vibe, if Gina was in her sixties, had worry lines, and was addicted to strawberry cheesecake. Don't get me wrong, despite Ma's full figure, she was beautiful. Her hair had stayed mostly brunette and she had what Josie called a "provocative" face. She wore the same gold crucifix she'd worn since her first communion.

"Is everything okay?" I asked.

"I'm fine, and so is Dad." I never asked about him, but she'd always been determined to insert him into our conversations. She was not apologetic about it, either. "*You* may wish he didn't exist, but I sure don't," she once said, shrugging.

She exhaled a long, hard funnel of smoke, then tapped ash into the old yellow ashtray.

"So, here it is, Tony. I'm just going to come out and say it. I've been good. I've been sympathetic, but I can no longer take the estrangement between you and Papa. Twenty years is too long. It stops now!"

I sputtered. "What? Not my fault, I—"

She index-finger silenced me. "Not your fault? At this point, it certainly is. You only see him at Christmas and Thanksgiving and even then you barely acknowledge him. And you won't come over if he's here, so he has to go to the coffee shop and sit by himself like a refugee until you leave. Why do you still hold onto this anger?"

"You know exactly why, Ma. He abandoned us. He was hardly ever home. He did a number on you, on all of us. End of friggin' story!"

"Not the end, son. Never the end. I want our family back before I die. And that includes your papa. Like it or not, he will always be your father."

I angrily crossed my arms. I wasn't going to budge on this.

My mother shook her head. "The day you quit racing was the day you grew cold toward Papa. Year after year, colder and colder! Yes, he deserved your anger, no question. But you had no right to mentally torture him for twenty years!"

"*Mentally torture?* He's the one who mentally tortured us!" I was astounded that my mother still couldn't see the truth.

Ma gave me a stern look. "Do you want to know the real reason your father wasn't around?"

"The real reason? You already told me. He had a gambling problem, he had debts to pay. Old news."

"Partly," she said, tapping the table. "But that's all I told you because you didn't want to hear anything else. But now you're going to hear what *I* have to tell you." Ma rarely got mad, but now she had that look that would make an Italian kid sit extra-tall and mind his manners.

"Think Back. What else do you remember about Papa's absence?"

I bristled. "*You* drove me to hockey, soccer, and the race track, and *you* cheered me on. *You* made sure we did our homework, our chores. Dad was never there. The only thing he ever did with us was go to Mass." I scoffed. "As if somehow God would forgive him."

"You listen to me, Tony, and you listen good. Papa wanted to be part of the family, but he couldn't."

I just snorted.

She looked angrier than ever, but there was suspicious moisture in her eyes.

"Just because your Papa was terrible with money doesn't mean he wasn't a good man with a good heart. He still is!"

My anger boiled over. "A good man? A good heart? Stop defending him, Ma. Why can't you accept that you married a—?" I stopped myself before I called my mother's husband a really bad name.

"He *does* have a good heart," she insisted. "And in their own sick way, so do Beppe and Toto. Otherwise, they would have busted Papa's kneecaps a long time ago."

I'd love to bust their kneecaps.

"Look, Papa doesn't want you to know what I'm about to tell you. He was always ashamed of what you and Josie would think of him. But you're not kids anymore and it's not fair to him, the way you've carried on."

"Beppe and Toto were country boys, back home," she continued. "They grew up idolizing the big city mobsters in Sicily and Agrigento, silly idiots, and when they immigrated to Hamilton, they played the part."

She tapped out more ash. "Beppe was the oldest, the toughest, and the smartest, so he ran the show. Believe me, they didn't run drugs or guns. I'd have known, because I kept close tabs on them all those years. I wanted to know exactly what your father was mixed up in. That bunch were terrified of the Musitano and Papalia families, so they stayed under their radar and just ran off-track betting—nothing over

$100, most of the time. Unfortunately, when it was a personal friend like your Dad, they upped the limit, sometimes a lot. Their customers were discreet, most of the bets placed in Beppe's kitchen."

Ma had cast a spell on me. I listened, despite my bitterness.

"Basically, your papa and the rest of them were a bunch of cocky young men, foolish and in love with a corrupt dream. Sometimes, they were dangerous, too, but you already knew that."

I scoffed. "I figured out most of this crap years ago! You should have been up front about this from the start, instead of covering for him!"

"Tony, I made a promise to your papa I wouldn't say anything. But last year he said it didn't matter anymore. That it might be better if you and Josie knew the truth about his addiction, then maybe both of you would go easier on him."

"Yeah, right."

Her words struck a nerve. Yes, my father hurt himself with his addiction, but he'd also ruined our family life. Was I supposed to feel sorry for him?

"When you were about ten, I came this close to leaving him."

How many times had I imagined that exact scenario, when I was angry and hurt by the chaos my father had inflicted on us? The thing is, I never believed it would really happen!

Ma nodded, grim-faced. "Behind my back, he tried to take out a second mortgage. But your Aunt Elena worked at the bank and she told me about it. It was the only time I slapped your papa." She blinked back a few tears. "He felt so bad the next day he went to one of those Gamblers Anonymous meetings. Beppe and Toto gave him a ride there. Ironic, huh? They didn't gamble. They were smart that way." She sounded bitter.

So, dirtbags Beppe and Toto were compassionate and full of love for their fellow dirtbag, Dad? Touching.

"By the time Papa beat his gambling habit, you had no love left for him. You were engaged to Angela and ready to leave your father behind you."

I took a deep breath to steel myself and asked a question Josie and I agonized over for years, but in light of this new info, it felt like the right moment. "Was he unfaithful to you, Ma? Sorry, I just figured since he was away so much, he...might have been tempted."

She squashed her cigarette butt in the ashtray, lit up another one, and exhaled more blue haze, avoiding my eyes.

"Papa was like a lot of men back then. Out at strip clubs. Easy women everywhere. But I knew they meant nothing to him. He told me every day he loved me and I believed him. I still do. And if he did stray, I don't need to know."

I felt the old disgust. Now I definitely didn't feel sorry for estranging him. That fucker Frank Valentini deserved it!

"Your father worked hard to raise a family. And he never missed a day of work."

"That doesn't make up for what he did to us! Besides, how can you love someone you can't trust?"

"I knew Papa wasn't very trustworthy, but my heart didn't care. When I fell for him, I fell hard, and my heart ran the show. That's how love is. I think you already understand that, deep down."

This was excruciating. Private, emotional stuff—the kind of stuff I could barely handle on a good day. But I needed to hear more. And I had my own things to unload.

"He never deserved you, Ma. End of story!"

"Enough with your 'end of story', Tony!" she roared. "You always say that! End of story, end of story! Her passion was disturbing. She flung out her hands. "When you were a boy, you convinced yourself Beppe was a mafia kingpin. And you were obsessed with the newspaper, reading anything you could about Hamilton mobsters, always scanning for evidence of Papa and Beppe and Toto. But, of course, you didn't find them, because they *weren't* big time mobsters." She looked heart-broken. "You were so convinced, Tony. And so scared. You still are."

That one hurt, I gotta say. "No, Ma, I'm not scared, and whether they're small-time crooks or straight outta The Godfather, it doesn't change anything. They're corrupt assholes, and Dad is one of them. And I know there's something else you're not telling me! I can feel it!"

Ma was angry. "You don't know what you don't know! And don't speak to me like that, Antonio!"

I opened my mouth to go off again, but she jabbed her finger at me. "After your big race, you're going to learn something very serious about your Papa. And you'll take it like a man, understand me? And no more end of story nonsense." Her lower lip began trembling. "You'll do that for me, won't you?"

I shrugged. There wasn't much I wouldn't do for my mother, but I didn't have to like it.

"*Everyone* deserves a second chance," she said. "*Everyone* deserves forgiveness. Remember the Lord's Prayer: 'And forgive us our transgressions, as we forgive those who transgress against us.' Forgive others or you won't be forgiven on Judgement Day."

Thinking madly, I examined the grease under my fingernails. Ma was still a staunch Catholic. Lately, some of the stuff I'd grown up with was looking more relevant to me. The hymns, the prayers, the priest's homilies—sometimes they hit the nail on the head, like they were written just for me. Besides, I wasn't exactly Mr. Perfect myself. But my bitterness ran very, very deep.

"If Giorgio loses," I said, "will *you* be able to forgive Dad for destroying your retirement? For forcing you to sell the house and live in a shithole apartment?"

"I'd live in a tent, if it meant spending the rest of my life with your papa!" She pounded the table. "I want my family back! You, Josie, Papa, and me. Before I die! That's all I care about!"

I heaved back in my chair. I'd heard enough. I'd had enough. Lord's Prayer or not, after Dad's big reveal I was forever done with him.

Ma deflated, and her expression went flat. She checked her watch. "Time to leave, Tony," she said, in a cold voice. "Papa will be home soon."

Silently, I headed out the kitchen and down the stairs, pulled on my shoes, and stormed out the door. Hell would freeze over first.

Chapter 16

WEDNESDAY, SEPTEMBER 21, 10:45 a.m.

It was four days until The Special.

Our Service manager, Jeff Beaton, swung open the waiting room door and cried, "Valentini, you have visitors!"

Visitors?

I glanced over the hood of the Honda I was working on at my co-worker, Sue. "This better be good," I grumped. "People know not to bug me at work."

"Maybe it's the folks from The Price is Right," she joked.

"Haha, very funny, Proenneke." It was a running joke between us. Sue knew I had a secret fantasy to be on that show. Secret was the operative word. It was an embarrassing little dream.

She laughed and went back to work under a Ford Focus.

I cleaned my greasy hands on a rag and headed to the waiting room, praying it wasn't bad news. There'd been more than enough of that, lately.

Maybe it was Donny, yipped up on a new idea. Once he'd showed up trying to sell me on becoming his business partner. Some guy had given him a deal on three giant boxes of multivitamins shaped like the Pope. "You can sell them at your church," he urged me. "Catholic vitamins!"

Instead of my nutty friend, I found two guys I used to know really well, waiting for me at the Service Counter. The years had carved lines in their faces. They had become middle-aged men. Like me.

My nerves kicked in, a delayed reaction.

Everything I thought I'd say if I ever I saw them again vanished from my brain. I was that tongue-tied with shock and nervousness, I couldn't speak for a moment,

But instead of looking angry and bitter, they were actually smiling, and not sarcastically, either.

Fuck it, I told myself, *pull it together, idiot!*

"Hoffy! Luke!" We exchanged handshakes. "Let's step outside," I said. We needed privacy. I told Jeff I needed a five-minute break.

We parked ourselves in front of a row of lawnmowers. The sun was shining and the parking lot was hopping. A chill wind reminded me that summer had died.

"Wow, been a long time, guys," I said. When were they going to start reaming me out?

"Too long," Hoffy agreed.

Larry Hoffman lit up a smoke. He'd gotten pudgy, and his dated brown slacks and blue sports jacket weren't doing him any favours. I knew that I'd packed on the beef, too, but Luke Ranger was still lean and muscular.

"Definitely," he said. He had a "Christ is King" tee under his shirt.

Both men wore Hermonville Raceway baseball caps. They'd been a year ahead of me at Irondale, and I hadn't gotten to know them until our Grade Eleven/Twelve split auto class, where we'd gotten along like a house on fire.

They'd been my teammates when I'd been the Prodigy. Larry had provided the car, thanks to a generous donation from his dad, Bud Hoffman. Mr. Hoffman owned a lucrative Ford dealership on the west Hamilton Mountain. Luke had wrenched on the car. We were a great unit.

I'd meant to track them down to thank them for everything they'd done for me, but I'd always found a reason to chicken out.

I hadn't seen them since I'd quit. When I'd told them I wasn't going to race again, they'd freaked out. For six months, they'd begged me to re-consider but fatherhood had trumped everything. Finally, the guilt of turning them down, week after week, got to be too much, so I blocked their phone numbers. I felt like a bag of shit for doing it but it had worked. I never heard from them again.

Until today.

I took a deep breath. "I'm sorry I let you guys down," I said. "I've owed you guys an apology for years."

"We didn't come here for an apology," Hoffy said, playfully shoving me. "We came to wish you well. We hear you're helping Giorgio Santucci break his curse."

Of course, the Hermonville gossip mill would have been on the case from my first night at the raceway.

"Well, uh, thanks, guys. I appreciate that. I'll take all the well wishes I can get." I wondered if they knew even half of what I was up against.

A customer was glaring at me through the window, obviously wondering why I wasn't inside fixing his Honda. But he'd have to wait. I wasn't about to ditch out on Hoffy and Luke. I owed them some time.

"What are you up to these days, Luke?" I asked.

"Divorced," he said, smiling weakly. "Two boys. Shared custody."

"Sorry, man."

"Shit happens," he said. "Gotta roll with the punches, right?"

"Where are you wrenching these days?"

"Fat Car Auto in Binbrook. On weekends, I wrench on Billy Drummond's car at Ohsweken."

Ohsweken Speedway was a popular race track southwest of Hamilton, down near Middleport. I'd raced there a lot as a teen.

"Drummond, eh? Nice! He's ranked fifth in the province." I'd kept up on all the regional racers, Giorgio included.

"You still in the car biz?" I asked Hoffy.

"Yep," he said flatly, none too thrilled with the business he'd inherited from his dad. He paused. "Tone, we know the real reason you ditched out, okay? And we totally understand. Right, Luke?"

"Right."

"The *real* reason?" I said, trying not to sound irritated.

Hoffy nodded. "Last week, we were at Tim's and some guy named Donny Love saw us wearing our Hermonville caps, so he plopped down beside us and yabbered on about racing and you—mostly you—and your relationship with your dad."

Of course he fucking did!

"The guy was a total motormouth," Luke laughed. "We couldn't get a word in."

"Yep, that's Donny. Soon to be an *ex*-friend."

"He said he wrote that "Making Steven Famous" column in the paper," Hoffy said. "And a book with the same name?"

"Yep." I was clenching my jaw so hard, it hurt.

"Actually," Luke said, "I found that column pretty entertaining. Although I could tell most of it was complete bullshit."

"Try *total* bullshit," I said. "Bullshit is Donny's middle name."

Hoffy pulled a face. "An unsung hero on a motorcycle, saving people in Kazikstan? Yeah, right."

"I liked it," Luke laughed. "Clint Eastwood in a poncho, rescuing folks. Who cares if it was bullshit? It was inspiring." He shook his head with regret. "Too bad it didn't last."

"We went to the concert," Hoffy added. "I thought it would be shit, but, honestly, it blew us away. Right, Luke?"

"Yeah. It was amazing. That Maurice guy sure is talented."

After that concert, Maurice Coquin had been featured on talk shows and done a tour in Japan and Korea. That weird night had jump-started his career.

"I don't remember seeing you guys there," I said.

"We saw you with your wife," Luke offered, "but we weren't sure how you'd react, so we kept our distance."

I thrust my hand through my hair. "Aw, shit. Sorry, man."

"All in the past," Hoffy said. "We're good, OK?"

Jeff swung out the door looking cranky. "Tony, need you back in here."

"Yeah, yeah," I grumbled. "Like I ever take a break." I lowered my voice. "He seriously needs to lighten the fuck up."

"Same old Tony," Luke smirked.

Hoffy focussed on me with purpose. "So, Tone, what are your plans after Giorgio?"

"Plans? No plans. Work. Be a dad. The usual. Why?"

"When you're ready, *if* you're ready, I'll buy us a car and we can team up again."

Heat spread down the core of my body. I seriously hadn't seen this coming. I'd expected to be bawled out, but instead I'd gotten an offer I could barely refuse.

Luke looked sad now. "Tone, working with you and Hoffy were the best days of my life, man."

"Those *were* great days," I said, sighing against the guilt I was feeling. "Awesome days."

Hoffy said, "Donny told us that, after the Steven Dundee madness, you and a buddy were going to invest in a car and race again. Is that true?"

That buddy had been Steven.

"Yeah," I said, feeling sheepish. "the concert got me hepped up. Thought I could go back in time and re-live the dream. But then I smartened up."

Jeff whipped opened the door. "Valentini!" He wasn't going to take no for an answer.

"I'm coming!"

I faced my old team mates. I realized how much I'd missed them. How much I missed *us.* And I was touched they'd forgiven me.

"Think about what I said, okay, Tone?" Hoffy said. "No pressure. But if and when you're ready, so are we."

I nodded. I just hoped they wouldn't be too disappointed when they realized I wasn't going to change my mind.

"Good luck Saturday," Luke said, offering his hand.

We pulled each other into a half-hug, and Hoffy and I slapped each other on the back.

They waved as they climbed into Hoffy's spanking new Mustang.

Knowing my old teammates had forgiven me made me feel light as a feather. But as I turned back to the service center door, the glass reflected the flash of a camera.

"What the fuck!" I cried.

As I spun around, the Datsun tore away, the muffler making a death-rattle.

Roaring, I took my steel-toed work boot to the garbage can, sending it flying into the path of an old guy on a scooter. He just missed it, but trash scattered all over the parking lot. Jeff came pounding out of the store, red-faced and angry. By the time I finished apologizing to the old guy, picking up all the trash and righting the garbage can, I'd attracted quite a big audience. They were fascinated by the angry maniac in coveralls.

Filled with shame, I kept my head down.

Chapter 17

MY MANAGER DID NOT ream me out in front of customers or co-workers, thank God. He saved the blasting until we got into his office, but I bet the folks on the other side of the store could hear him. He had some lungs on him.

The only reason he didn't fire me was that I really was his best mechanic. I apologized—sincerely—and headed back into the service bay. Toward the end of my shift, the day got worse, if you can imagine that.

"Valentini!" Jeff bellowed from the waiting area door. "Phone call!"

Shit. We were not supposed to take calls at work, not unless it was a real emergency.

Jeff scowled when he handed me the phone.

"Hello?"

It was Beppe, dammit, in full *Godfather* mode. "I got an offer you can't refuse, Tony Valentini."

I turned away from Jeff and the last customer and lowered my voice. "And what flippin' offer would that be?"

"You're gonna race in tomorrow tonight's 15-lap Last Chance Special. And you're gonna win, so you can race with Giorgio in The Special, the thirty-five lap Main, the Big Meatball."

I was gobsmacked. Race? In the Last Chance Special? Shit. I must've missed the "Offer Your Favourite Addict Some Heroin Day' announcement that morning. "Look, Beppe, Giorgio's got this. I'd only get in his way."

"You don' understand, Tony. Giorgio's got no confidence. He's been pacing around the house all day, biting his fingernails. The doctor's techniques don' work no more. He says only the Prodigy can save him now. You're his lucky rabbit foot, he says. *You're* the cure for my Giorgio."

This was all so whack-job crazy that my head was spinning.

"Beppe, *sir*, I haven't raced in twenty years! I'm rusty as hell. Trust me, I'll just make an ass of myself and mess up Giorgio's chances."

"You already shedda' the rust. I *seen* you dice with Giorgio. I know, you sometimes let him win. I'm not stupid. God gave me eyes to see. And not only that, I know why you done it."

I didn't trust myself to respond.

"Yeah, you tanked on purpose to make Giorgio more confident, and it worked. And that's why you gonna win tonight, so you can race with him at The Special and make him even more confident. Only you can do that Tony. He trusts you. He needs you. Capeesh?"

"Giorgio won his last three races, including the Rockin' Sprint Tour at Ohsweken, because Dr. Hotz cured him. He just has pre-race jitters. That's perfectly normal. He's got this, Beppe. Trust me!" I was flying by the seat of his pants, Donny Love style.

There was a noticeable pause. "Do you love your parents?"

His barely-veiled threat stopped me cold.

"So, I will see you Thursday night, Tony Valentini."

After he hung up, I stood frozen for a few minutes. Jeff finally ended my paralysis. "Get back to work, Tony. Just do your damn job, will ya?"

So that's what I ended up doing. I did my damn job.

Chapter 18

THURSDAY, SEPTEMBER 22, 8:00 p.m.

I got behind the wheel and won the Last Chance Special, to keep my family safe—even my crappy, undeserving father.

From the time the green flag dropped, I found myself operating on pure instinct, barely aware of the cars around me. There was a surreal quality to the night. Within the first minute or two I couldn't even see my competitors. But the car ran like a dream, and when the checkered flag waved, I suddenly woke up.

Shivers like high voltage had buzzed through my bones.

Giorgio was the first to greet me in the pit with a bear hug. "You're in the Special, Tony!" he cried. "Listen to that crowd! They loved having you back on the track. And now we get to race together. Isn't that joyous?"

Now that he'd mentioned it, I noticed the rowdy audience was still revved up. It was nicer to hear them cheering for me than I liked to admit.

"Way to get 'er done!" Tanner cried. "Tight in the turns and magic on the lever!"

I expected Randy to chime in but then it occurred to me I hadn't seen him yet tonight.

The thing is, I had known I'd win. The minute I'd put my hands on the wheel, I'd just known. I wasn't going to share that little gem with anyone, though. No one else would really understand. They'd just think I was an egotistical ass. But I wasn't. I'd just had a moment of clarity. I was exactly where Fate wanted me to be.

Giorgio grinned at me. "You were amazing. And now you're in The Special with me. And I'll be super confident." He clasped his hands. "Tony Valentini, sir, you are Heaven sent!" He looked past my shoulders and his eyes went wide. "Time for you to get famous!"

I turned and saw the same Channel 11 reporter and her camera man from days of the Steven Dundee madness. I shuddered, remembering the bullshit I'd spewed to her. Crap about opening up a new race way with Steven and buying a race car. Hell, we'd all been infected by Donny's Attention Whore Virus back then. Today, I promised myself, I would not be a fool.

"We're here with Tony Valentini, aka the Prodigy, who has just won the 15-lap Last Chance Special after coming out of a twenty-year retirement." She pointed the microphone at me. "How does it feel to be the comeback kid?"

I wished Norb were there to blast me with his Invisiblator. I mean, who calls a forty-one-year-old a *kid*? Or a Prodigy, for that matter? "There *is* no comeback, ma'am. After The Special, win or lose, the Prodigy's retiring for good." I cringed. Only an a-hole would call himself the Prodigy! *Fucking camera!*

"At the height of your career, you had seven wins in single year," she countered cheerfully. "An unbroken record. Very impressive, Tony." She smiled perfect white teeth for the camera then flashed them at me. "So, Prodigy, how does it feel to be a Canadian racing legend?"

"I don't feel anything," I stammered, feeling the way Giorgio must have when he drifted out of his body.

She asked more questions, but as the implications of my win started to really sink in, I clammed up. Frustrated, she hustled away to find someone more chatty to interview.

Tanner nodded approvingly. "You still got it, buddy."

Giorgio had been soaking up the interview, obviously looking for me to be his press-handling role model, poor bastard.

"I got nothing." I was feeling pretty grim now.

"Someone's been eating their Lucky Charms," Giorgio said, playfully poking my shoulder.

"Man, I love Lucky Charms," Tanner chimed in.

Giorgio was thrilled to hear that tidbit. "How can you not, right?"

When they started their fist-bumping shit, I turned to hit the road, but the mobsters up in the stands caught my attention. Beppe was power-puffing his stogie, studying a racing form, and Doughboy had his fingers in his mouth, whistling like a police siren. Either he was happy for me or showing off, and Dad, well, Dad *looked* happy. And he *never looked* happy. The reason for his good mood was obvious. After all, I was in the Special with Giorgio, and because of that, Giorgio might just win and clear Dad's debt.

Now feeling bitter, I was half way past my sprint car, when Randy Rocket slid out from under it. He had on coveralls and was gripping an oil rag and a socket wrench. It didn't occur to me to wonder why he'd bother with a post-race inspection.

Then I noticed an angry red mark on his cheek. It looked like a burn. "Are you okay, Randy?"

He wagged his finger at me. "Engine burn. No biggie. Be cool."

He slid back under my car.

If I'd been a nicer person, I might have grabbed the first aid kit and put some salve on his cheek. However, I was feeling done with everybody by then. And, let's face it, I wasn't that nice a guy. I had a leather heart, most of the time.

Down the way, a CHML radio reporter was asking Giorgio how he felt today, after re-earning his nickname, The Second Place Slider. I have to hand it to him—Giorgio put a positive spin on everything. Despite his babyish oddness, he actually *was* a nice person.

My cell phone rang. It was Beppe, in the stands, waving at me with his phone pressed to his ear. It was hard to hear him over the crowd.

"You raced well, kid. But tomorrow you make my Giorgio win. Anyone tries to beat him, you finish him off." He made a gunshot sound. "Yes."

What the hell? Did he want me to shoot a driver?

"Whatever it takes, capeesh?"

I shuddered. Did this psycho seriously expect me to do that? I didn't own a damn gun. Even if I had, I would never do that. Never.

He laughed, a dirty creepy laugh. "After the race, we celebrate at my place. You bring your family. You meet *my* family. Champagne. Dinner. The works!"

Then he just hung up.

My fear and anger had to go somewhere. I hauled Randy out from under the car. "This car has to be in top shape for tomorrow, Randy! No taking it apart, no games. And the kid's car better be the best wrenching you've ever done in your life, hear me? He *has* to win, got it?"

He double-tapped his nose.

I couldn't let go of him. All my terror had hijacked me. I found myself shaking him. "What are you really hiding from, asshole?" I raged in his ear. "What are you running from?" I vaguely registered the sound of gasps as I got my fingers under his left eye-bandage and yanked, but then, with shockingly powerful hands, Giorgio grabbed my wrists and held me still.

Randy's whole body was trembling. The bandage half-hung on the top of his cheek. I could see his pale blue eye exposed to the world and filled with tears. With a hiccup of a sob, he jammed the bandage back up over his naked eye.

My arms dropped like wet noodles. Exhausted, I plopped down on my haunches.

"I'm sorry," I moaned. I thought I might vomit. I looked up to find a ring of distraught onlookers. "Sorry, everyone." Then I realized my wife and daughter were standing there, staring.

Oh, dear God. My daughter had seen me attacking a mentally ill guy?

I staggered to my feet, feeling like I'd been hit by a truck. Randy slid back under the car on his creeper, out of sight. A mole in his hole.

Giorgio was patting my back. "It's all going to work out, my friend. Tomorrow will be merry."

I got back to my feet. I'd barely heard Giorgio—I was so dazed and upset from witnessing Randy's meltdown. I looked everywhere but he'd disappeared.

I found myself avoiding Angie's gaze, Angel's gaze. Even talking to Giorgio right now was preferrable to facing them in my shame. I just shook my head at Giorgio.

"Ye of little faith, Tony Valentini," he laughed. "How about we go to the clubhouse and share a cold glass of milk and talk about your feelings?"

"How about straight bourbon and we don't talk at all."

He looked like I'd promised him a miracle. "Deal!"

Coward that I was, I would go drink with the kid, rather than have the conversation that was coming with my wife and daughter. I could see them, out of the corner of my eye, pushing through the crowd, heading for me. I couldn't read the expression on Angie's face.

Then I noticed him.

Beyond the thinning crowd, at the edge of the parking lot. Walker. His movie camera was pointed at me like the eye of a deadly spider.

"Daddy, what's wrong?" Angel cried, seeing the sudden rage on my face.

"Call a cab and go home!" I barked at Angie, and I took off, pounding toward him.

I could hear Angie and Giorgio yelling behind me but I ignored them. I had a man to kill!

I sprinted through the clubhouse and weaved through the crowd in the parking lot. My belly was bobbling up and down so hard it hurt.

But why wasn't Walker running away? Even from a distance, I could make out the smirk on his face!

My rage drove me forward. At some point, fans around me picked up on the drama unfolding in the parking lot. It was just their kinda fun.

"No one fucks with the Prodigy!" a woman behind me screeched.

"Go get 'em champ!" someone yelled supportively.

Then actual chanting started up, "Prodigy! Prodigy! Prodigy!"

I didn't have the breath to yell at them to can it. I hadn't sprinted like that since my mid-twenties, when I'd run out onto Steel Street to save Frankie, who'd suddenly decided it would be fun to chase a bird on his tricycle.

Despite my heroic efforts, just as I got to within ten yards of the guy, Walker rubbered and won. He'd screeched his shitbox car out of the parking lot, leaving me wheezing in his dust.

In between hacking coughs, I yelled, "Sonofabitch!" and gave his rearview mirror double middle fingers.

I lurched through the crowd, who'd shifted from bloodthirsty to sympathetic, toward the van.

"Good try, dude. You almost had him," a long-haired teen offered. His shirt said, "In my defense, I was left unsupervised."

I was vibrating. Sweating in places I didn't normally sweat.

I was also floating outside of myself, Giorgio-style, watching myself the way Giorgio said he did when he was super anxious. It really was a horrible feeling, but how could I have known? How could anyone, unless they experienced it first hand? The accumulated stress of the last few months had totally skinned my nerves.

My mind shifted back to Walker filming me. I felt violated.

Re-energized by a fresh wave of fury, I peeled the van out of the parking lot, scattering a few people out of the way. I ripped out onto Carlisle Road too fast. Way too fast. The van tipped up onto two wheels for just a moment.

I was able to right it. When the wheels slammed the pavement, the van shook. My eight track tapes bucked off the dash and tumbled down onto the floor.

I smashed the pedal to the metal.

On top of that, I made the bad decision to call Donny, as I raced down Highway 6, going well over the speed limit. I made him give me Walker's address. "Call the guys and all of us meet there in forty!" I yelled.

I punched the first tape I could lay my hands on into the stereo. It blasted Alice Cooper's "No More Mr. Nice Guy". Soon, I was cooking up evil fantasies of torturing Walker. But God must've decided enough was enough, because steam began hissing out from under the hood.

Cussing a blue streak, I skidded onto the shoulder and popped the hood. Someone had taken the radiator cap! I screamed Dave Walker's name so loud that a flock of Canada Geese flew up out of the field beside me, honking in shock. I just about peed myself.

I scanned the dark highway and fields around me. Was he lurking, watching his evil plan unfold? I prayed that plan didn't involve a butcher knife.

I called the CAA to send a tow truck, then Donny to cancel D-Day at Walker's house.

To top it off, I kicked the front car tire so hard I just about broke my big toe. My toe felt squishy with blood.

I hobbled to the passenger side and slid down the door to sit on the ground. The pain in my foot had dulled my rage enough to remind me of my own shitty, stupid behaviour.

A while later, a cab pulled over. My girls peered out at me. And I'd never been so glad to see them.

Chapter 19

"Honey, I'm worried about you." Angie was studying me across the breakfast table. Angel was still in her room.

Last time she'd said that to me had been a few weeks ago, when I'd been in the can, scripting an argument with Dad; it turns out I'd been shouting. Over the years, she'd suggested more than once that I get counselling, but I never did.

"Why?" I nervously stood up and went to pour some coffee. I already knew why. I rejoined her at the table, waiting for her to unravel me. We'd gone to bed in silence last night, our bedroom thick with tension. She'd tossed and turned as much as I had. I knew she'd unload this morning, and she had every right to.

"Do you understand what you did to Randy yesterday?" she said. "You bullied him, Tony, in front of Angel, in front of everyone else, for that matter. What's gotten into you?" She sighed. "You scared me, Tony."

I was swimming in shame. "I know, Angie. Believe me, I feel sick about it."

"And you went after that Dave Walker like a complete maniac. Why? Just because he was filming you? Yeah, it's definitely annoying, but it doesn't warrant violence. What if you'd caught him? What if you hurt him so badly you ended up in jail? What would Angel think of you? What would happen to our family?" Her bottom lip was quivering. Yeah, my wife was upset.

I could barely breathe now.

She leaned forward. "You have big-time control issues, Tony. You've instructed your dad, your friends—everyone, actually, just what they're allowed to say about the estrangement. Heaven help any of us when we bring it up to you. Now you've bullied poor Randy, who's obviously mentally ill, and you chased Walker because it drives you crazy you can't lock him up in a box. You even kicked a garbage can at work, and last night you almost broke your toe, kicking the tire."

"I'm sorry," I croaked.

Hearing our daughter up in the bathroom, she lowered her voice. "And you lock your feelings in your heart so I only know half of you. That really hurts, Tony, because I feel you don't trust me. And yet, *I* tell you everything." She wiped her eyes with a tissue.

"I love you more than anything, Angie, you gotta know that." She shook her head like she didn't believe me. That broke my heart.

She was right. I had serious control issues. Deep down, I'd always known I had, but I hadn't understood just how much that affected her. I felt even worse knowing she hadn't challenged me on it until now. How long had she suffered this part of our marriage in silence?

"You deserve better, Angie. I'll see Dr. Hotz when this is all over. I promise."

Chapter 20

9 P.M.

It was one of the most deranged things I'd ever seen.

An hour earlier, I'd easily won the first 15 lap feature and Giorgio had snagged second, no surprise. Four grand for me and three for him. We were having a blast, giddy with excitement. The stands were packed. The smell of methanol and cigarette smoke and barbecued meat filled the air all the way out to the track. Smells of old. I realized how much I'd missed them.

We were waiting to be push-started for the second feature. Giorgio was a stone's throw behind me. As Joe Messina drove his truck up to push me, I was leaning out of my car to wave good luck to Giorgio when, from far down the track, a blob shot towards me like a splatter of slow-motion solder.

My biggest fear was happening.

When he got closer, I realized Randy was wearing a shiny foundry suit, but not one from this world. It randomly sprouted wires and cables, the biggest one thick as a python, with a big clamp on the end. It stuck out of the top of a round space helmet. A circuit board on a chain dangled over Randy's chest. It looked fucked-up and old, likely ripped out of an old computer or a dumpster. The wires vibrated in the air like electric snakes. Like Space Medusa.

As he came closer, I could hear him ranting about electromagnetic waves slowing Giorgio's car. I finally realized that Randy's illness had a mind of its own, and there was no penetrating or controlling it. It wasn't taking no for an answer. Randy was going to get Giorgio disqualified.

But as he dove under Giorgio's car, trying to wiggle his way under the hood, I launched out of my car, anyway. Giorgio was already on him by the time I got there. He had Randy by the ankle, slowly dragging him out. Randy had dug his gloved hands into the dirt and was kicking and screaming inside his silver spacesuit, making me feel sick to my stomach, but he was no match for powerful Giorgio.

"Randy, it's okay!" Giorgio cried, rolling him onto his back. Randy struggled like a possessed hot dog wrapped in tinfoil.

"I beat my anxiety!" Giorgio reassured him. His face was full of pity. "So you don't have to do this anymore, OK? I can win on my own now. I'll prove it to you. I promise." He waved Dr. Hotz down from the stands.

The horrible sounds Randy was making inside his helmet raked shivers down my back. Behind his helmet visor, I caught a glimpse of his eyes. He'd ripped off his bandages! What I saw in them was like slaughterhouse terror.

His panic was infecting me. I felt almost dizzy with it.

Randy clenched and un-clenched his fists in his big gloves. "Must! Stop! The evil waves!" he screamed repeatedly. He started punching his helmet. Giorgio pressed his arms down to the dirt.

Two Track officials had hurried over to see what the hell was going on. The Grand Marshall was waving a red flag. Everything had ground to a halt.

"You must be so hot in this suit," Giorgio said in a gentle voice. "Let me take your helmet off." Surprisingly, Randy let him. As soon as his face was exposed, he squeezed his eyes shut. I knew that he was desperately trying to protect that most vulnerable part of himself.

Next thing I knew, Dr. Hotz was down on her knees beside him, consoling him, and Joe Messina was doing crowd control to give Randy and the doctor space. The racers and their crews had come to watch. I doubted Hermonville Raceway had ever seen anything like this.

"I can't imagine what you're going through, Randy," Dr. Hotz said softly. "It must be so hard. But please know I'm here for you. I'm going to help you." She nodded to the responders who carefully moved in. "We're going to the ER, Randy. I'll ride with you."

Randy went limp. The four responders had to pick him up by his arms and legs to carry him off the track. They loaded him onto a stretcher, then into the back of the ambulance and shuttled him away. The whole time he didn't put up a fight. Either he was cooperating or he'd gone catatonic.

Giorgio and I sagged with relief, but it took me more than a few minutes to come around, after all the traumatic drama. We gave each other an awkward hug, and the kid clapped me on the back. "Now he's going to get better. Just wait and see," he declared with total faith.

Shit, I sure hoped so.

Thirty minutes later, the green flag dropped. And Giorgio raced like I'd never seen him race before.

Chapter 21

SATURDAY, SEPTEMBER 24, 8:34 a.m.

Full of pre-race jitters, I forced down my breakfast. Angie had buried herself in *The Gazette*, letting me process my thoughts.

I'd had a good talk with Dr. Hotz over the phone last night. She'd told me Randy had been off his meds for eight months and had agreed to give them another try. Her colleague had filled out a prescription for him. "Once he gets enough into his system, he should balance out," she reassured me. I was relieved for the guy.

Last night, Giorgio had said Randy's crisis was the wake-up call he'd needed. How obsessing over something or somebody can make a person really sick. Like how he himself was always obsessing over gaining his father's approval. "Now I'm waking up, too," he'd said, in his usual cheerful way.

Of course, I thought about my own obsession with my father, how toxic my rage was, how estranging him had done such a number on me and my family. After this was over, I vowed to fix that, once and for all.

Giorgio was off to a great start to becoming his own man. He'd won the second feature without the security of Dr. Hotz in the stands. He realized he could win on his own now. He'd found a way to minimize his anxiety. It was just too bad Randy had missed that big moment.

Angel scooted down the hall into the kitchen. Her smile lit up the room.

Then a loud knock at the front door startled me so badly my fist hit the breakfast table, rattling cutlery and plates. I was back to being control-freak Tony.

"Better not be the friggin' Jehovah's Witnesses," I groused. With the state I was in, not even the Pope himself would've been welcome.

"Tony," Angie said, "relax, okay? They're just doing what they believe. No harm done."

"Bullshit," I grumbled.

She went to get up but Angel had already raced down the hallway.

"Tell them to hit the road!" I cried after her. "Same thing if it's The Weed Guy. Or Bell Telephone! If it's a leprechaun with a pot of gold let him in."

I could hear our daughter giggle. Better to be entertained by my bad mood than traumatized by it.

My wife lovingly squeezed my arm. She knew I was under tremendous pressure to help Giorgio win today. She gave me a reassuring smile, but I couldn't return it. I was too uptight and worried, and the smell of the eggs on my plate was making me queasy.

Late last night, the tow truck had dropped the van off in my driveway. Turns out Walker had screwed with a lot more than my radiator cap. I could have fixed it myself, but there was no time today.

"I have to be at the track at noon," I said to Angie. "I'll call a cab."

"Angelina and I are coming with you," she said. "And I'm not taking no for an answer. We love you and we're going to support you."

When the rubber hit the road, Angie was Team Tony all the way. And that made me the luckiest cat on the planet. Today, I needed her more than ever, and that was saying a helluva lot, because we'd been to Hell and back more than once.

To top it off, I saw how Dad's bullshit had done a number on her. She looked like death warmed over. The bags under her eyes were as bad as mine. It made me mad as fuck. My wife deserved peace, not chaos. *All your fault, Dad!*

I shifted in my seat. My toe throbbed. My joints ached worse than ever.

Our daughter screamed in the front hall.

Angie and I charged out of the kitchen. Angel ducked behind me, trembling. On the other side of the screen door was...*me*. Dressed in blue coveralls and work boots, resting bulldog face—unmistakably me! Talk about freaky! If Norbert Reingruber hadn't been standing beside him, I would have thrown open the door and pounded the guy.

"Now what are you idiots up to?" I eyed *me* suspiciously.

"Sorry, Tony," Norb said. "It's urgent."

"Who's this meatball pretending to be me?" I snapped at Donny. "Not fucking Walker, I hope!" I stepped out, blocking the door.

"Of course not," Donny chimed in, squeezing in between us. "We hired him so we can snare Walker."

Fake Me gave me a grin that was way too much like the one I saw in the mirror. *What the fuck?*

"Don't make him talk," Norb added. "If he has to talk, we have to pay extra."

John was nervously tapping his stupidly large shoe against the porch. It looked like a friggin' clown shoe! Had he completely lost it?

I stepped back, wary. What were these idiots planning? Knowing them, it would be a shit show.

"How?" I said. "How is this supposed to go down?"

Angie was just shaking her head, horrified at the sight of my double.

"Dad, he looks just like you," Angel gasped.

I turned around and gave her the most reassuring smile I could muster. "It's just like a cool Halloween costume, honey. Nothing to be scared of, OK?"

"So, here's the plan. We're going to go film Walker at his house," Donny said. "When he sees the three of us, and the fake *you*, he'll think you withdrew from the race. Meanwhile, you'll actually be at the track, racing in peace. Plus, we'll film the crap out of *him* and see how he likes it!" He beamed, like he'd invented the cure for cancer. "Ha! How do you like them apples, Walker!"

"Yeah," Norb echoed, "them apples!"

John shrugged. "It's not exactly Operation Desert Storm, but it might work, right?"

"For sure," Norb said, "and if he figures out the fake you is not really you and tries to take off in his car to go the track, well, good luck Walker-Shmocker!"

"Good luck, why, Norb?"

He peeled a baggie of sand out of his jeans pocket and held it up. "The old sand in the gas tank trick, right out of the Doughboy's playbook, right, Angelina?"

"Yesss!" she cried, excitedly. "You'd do that for me, Uncle Norb?"

"Two wrongs don't make a right," I said to her, even though I loved the idea of disabling Walker's crapmobile.

Norb tousled Angel's hair. "It's time we gave Walker a taste of his own medicine, see how he likes it."

My daughter nodded her head like a little castanet. She was so hopped on the thought of revenge, it was shocking!

"Guys, this all sounds so dangerous," Angie said, "and *wrong*." She threw me a worried look. "Tony, let the cops deal with Walker. He could have a weapon."

Fake me gave a little shudder and then grinned.

"Forget the cops," I said, "These guys will get him our way. And I doubt he has a weapon. Other than his frickin' camera."

Angie wasn't convinced.

"If he gets dangerous, honey," I said, "they promise they'll call the cops. Right, guys?" They nodded enthusiastically.

"You all better." She gave us all her steeliest look.

I assessed my double. The only thing off about him was his wrists. They were thin. I had thick wrists. Hopefully Walker wouldn't notice. "Pull your cuffs lower, man," I said.

This was a bad idea on many levels. But I didn't have time to consider any of them. Hopefully, my friends wouldn't fuck things up too badly. There's a first time for everything, right?

"Thanks, guys," I said hastily. "Do what you gotta do." I turned, but then a thought occurred to me. "Donny, how's your dad?"

His good mood evaporated. "Critical condition. The doctors don't really know which way he's gonna go, yet."

Norb patted Donny's back and John shoe-gazed.

"I'm sorry, man. Archie's in our prayers."

"Thanks, Tony," Donny said. "I really appreciate that."

We half-hugged, awkward but sincere, and then the boys headed off on their crazy mission.

My friends cared so much about me they'd hired an actor to keep me safe from Walker. And Donny was dealing with potentially losing his father, but he'd *still* come to my rescue.

Suspecting they'd always cared about me was one thing, but seeing such evidence of it was a horse of another colour. One day, hopefully a *long* time from now, I'd be burying one of these guys. When that day came, I'd be a basket case.

I actually began to blubber. Shit, this was *not* like me.

"Everything's going to be okay," Angie said, hugging me. "You're just overwhelmed, honey. It's all a lot."

"Why are you crying, Dad?" Angel asked, looking up at me. She looked scared and on the verge of tears, herself.

"Well, I just—I just realized how lucky I am to have good friends and a loving family."

"I love your friends, Dad," she said. "Even though they *are* super weird. Especially Uncle Norb."

We all laughed a little and hugged some more.

So, there I was, stressed out of my gourd before a do-or-die race, having had my first *It's a Wonderful Life* moment. Every Christmas Eve we watched that movie, and every time I'd pretend to fall asleep, and the girls would call me Scrooge. But what they didn't know was that I'd had to close my eyes, rein in all that emotion, or I would have sobbed like a little boy.

Some shrink would probably talk about my fear of emotional vulnerability coming from the instability and trauma in my childhood home, and *blah blah blah*, but tonight I really didn't care.

The time for tears was over.

I had bigger fish to fry.

Chapter 22

THE SETTING SUN SPARKLED in the track dust, but my mood was dark.

Against all odds, and for all the right and wrong reasons, this middle-aged wop from Stinky Town found himself competing in *the* prestigious end-of-year event at Hermonville Raceway. The Canadian Crate Nationals 35 Lap A-Main (aka *The Special*). I was shitting bricks.

I knew what Norb would say: *Hot diggity dog!*

"Only if we win, Norb," I mumbled to myself. "Then *triple* hot-diggity-dog."

I punched my thigh so hard it hurt. Everything that had gone down in the past two weeks had proved that I could have raced *and* been a good family man! Angela would have supported me! The feeling that I'd wasted years of my life sucked me down.

I rocked the regret hole for a good five minutes, deeper than ever. It took everything I had to yank myself out.

We parked in our assigned starting positions—Giorgio in second, me in fifteenth because I'd finished first in the Last-Chance Special. Tanner was in eighth.

From the press box above the stands, an announcer's voice boomed through the P.A. system. "All drivers at their right front! All crew in the back! Stand by for driver introductions!"

Crews crossed the track to be with their drivers.

Now my heart was really pounding.

I reminded myself that all three of my friends had demonstrated courage in the craziest of situations over the past two years. "You can do this," I told myself, feeling totally unconvinced.

Then, for some insane reason, Giorgio sprinted across the front straight and disappeared into the clubhouse.

"Where the hell's he going?" I shouted at Tanner.

"Probably the tacos he had at lunch!" he shouted back. "I told him to eat the steak and eggs instead but he wouldn't listen." He laughed good-naturedly, shaking his head.

This isn't fucking funny! If Giorgio didn't race, we'd *both* be screwed.

"Don't worry about your number one, Tony!" Tanner cried. "Giorgio shits like a jackrabbit on steroids! He'll be back in a jiff!"

A couple of drivers within earshot had a good laugh at that one.

I was sweating like a pig. One that *couldn't* fly.

"Ladies and gentleman!" the announcer roared. "How about a big hand for all the amazing sprint car drivers here today. Look at these badass Crates, out for their big night. We're going to witness some awesome racing tonight so, once again, let's hear it for the Special!"

The crowd went crazy. The announcer continued, "My good friends Ryan and Adam will give us the starting line-up for the 19th Annual Canadian Crate Nationals." Ryan and Adam looked to be young guys, probably radio and tv broadcasting students from Mohawk College.

"Here's your starting line-up for tonight's thirty-five lap main event!" Adam said. "Starting in the thirtieth spot, from Hermonville, in car 79, welcome Shane Parker!" As the kid continued and the crowd cheered, I let my attention wander.

I was choked up by who I saw in the stands.

The Village had shown. Lots of people I knew and some I loved. Some co-workers, Jimmy-the-barber, and a couple of guys whose cars I'd been repairing for decades. All of them were waving homemade banners, a few with crazy gold face paint in the colour of Giorgio's car. When they saw me staring up at them, they began chanting, "Tony, Tony, Tony!", louder and louder until they thundered like a jet engine. Why would anyone other than my family and a couple of friends come to support me? Maybe it was a sympathy cheer? Donny must have blabbed to everyone about the debt and rallied them to come.

The young announcer's voice startled me back to reality. He was doing that growling thing that race fans loved. "In fifteenth spot, from Hamilton, in car 49, winner of the Last Chance Special, the Comeback Kid, Tony the Prodigy Valentini!"

The cheering went deafening. Maybe they had me confused with Steve Kinser? Couldn't they see I was a middle-aged burn-out? I was going to let them down. It was inevitable!

I shook my head. Time to focus, Tony!

I scanned the track for Giorgio, but there was still no sign of him.

"Where is he?" I shouted at Tanner. He shrugged and shook his head, finally having the sense to look worried now. *Shit!*

"Hey, Prodigy!" cried a voice from behind. A young kid with red hair and freckles driving car 77. Couldn't have been more than eighteen. "What's your secret?"

I looked at him blankly.

"You know, how do you not race for like twenty years and suddenly you're great again?"

Was this kid yanking my chain. He looked sincere.

"I dunno," I called back. Lamest response ever. *Now leave me the fuck alone!*

He grinned stupidly at me and gave me a thumbs up.

The closer the announcer got to finishing, the sicker I felt. I hid the trembling of my hands by tucking them under my armpits. *I'm too old to race*, I thought. *My nerves can't handle this. And Giorgio will feel bad for me and then he'll screw up!*

The announcer boomed, "In second spot, from Greensborough—" He stopped cold. The place actually went silent. All eyes were glued to Giorgio's empty car. Had he passed out on the shitter? Dammit! There was no time to go check on him.

A murmuring had started up in the stands.

Two officials and Joe Messina hurried onto the track in a panic.

They passed Giorgio's ghost car.

Where the fuck are you, Giorgio? I pounded the hood of my car.

They stopped in front of me. "Where's Giorgio?" Messina asked, looking pissed.

"Tanner said he went to the shitter!" I blurted. "He should've been back by now!"

"We checked," Joe said. "He's not there. He's not anywhere."

"What?"

Joe waved at the press box.

The announcer cried, "Giorgio Santucci, please return to your car. You have one minute or you'll be disqualified!"

Boos shot up from the crowd.

Joe checked his watch.

We waited for what seemed an eternity.

But Giorgio didn't show.

And that's when Beppe bowled onto the track, his cigar jiggling out of his mouth like an old cock. He was wearing a beautifully tailored three-piece black suit, looking exactly how you'd expect the mob guy who controlled the track to look.

He crooked his finger and Joe and the officials hot-footed it over to him, far enough that I wouldn't be able to hear their conversation. But I wasn't having it. There was too much at stake!

I galloped over and joined them. "Look, Giorgio *has* to race! Or my parents are fucked!" I glared at Beppe.

His face hardened. He jabbed his middle sausage-finger into my chest so hard it hurt. He threw his *Godfather* shit into high gear. "I tell you what we're gonna do, *tough guy*. You gonna drive Giorgio's car, and you gonna *make* it win. Capeesh?"

"No, no fucking capeesh! That's not our deal!"

"We've discussed it," Joe said. "And because you qualified, you can drive in Giorgio's place, but you're gonna have to drive *his* car."

I fought to take in this horrible, fucked-up news. After a punishing second or two, I heard myself ask, "And start in second place, right?"

"No," one of the officials said, "in fifteenth place. What you earned."

My insides turned to gruel. *Fifteenth place? There was no way I could win from there.* I began pacing. I stopped abruptly. "Has a no-show ever happened before? It's unusual, so maybe you can adjust the rules this time, right?"

"Nope," the other official said. "Hasn't happened, ever. But that doesn't matter. All that matters is that you get to race in Giorgio's place. You win, Giorgio wins. Your parents win. End of story."

My temper finally woke up. "End of story, buddy? That's *my* fucking line!"

He shrugged me off. "You can't copyright an expression." Randy had said the same thing!

"The hell I fucking can't!"

It was a totally ridiculous thing to be in a rage about, I know, but I guess all the stress had made me kinda nuts.

How could Giorgio have abandoned me? Nice guys don't do that. Maybe someone had kidnapped him? Maybe he'd buckled under the stress and was getting drunk in a bar somewhere?

Everyone in the stands was on their feet. Ma's face looked tight with worry, but I was pretty sure the distress on Dad's face was fake. He probably just wanted everyone to think he actually cared about me.

"Fuck you, Dad!" I roared, jabbing double middle fingers at him. "*You* did this to me! You fucked me up! You fucked Ma up! You fucked Josie up! You ruined my racing career! You mother, fucking, selfish two-bit mafia, piece-of-shit asshole!"

Beppe and his crew stared in deathly silence.

My heart was a pounding meat-hammer.

"You want The Progeny?" I screamed at my fans, turbo-charged by rage, jabbing my finger at them. "I'll show you The Fucking Progeny!" I dove feet first into Giorgio's car.

Crews and officials cleared off the track at a signal from Messina.

I tightened my fists around the steering wheel as the push trucks bump-started us. We drove the oval track until the field shaped up. I could barely contain myself, I was so terrified of losing. Reluctantly, I dropped to my fifteenth spot.

Thank God I'd won the Last Chance Special. If I hadn't, Ma would have already hired a real estate agent and would probably be stocking up on dog food

The traditional fireworks display went off. AC DC's "Hell's Bells" blasted through the P.A. system, as we paraded our cars past the stands. The fans loved this part, and the drivers usually waved and gave them a thumbs-up. Tonight, I barely noticed any of it.

I kissed the crucifix around my neck, a comforting little ritual.

"Let's do this!" I urged myself. "Come on, you asshole! You got this!"

On the back stretch, by the time the pace car pulled off and the green flag had dropped, I felt like I had a gun pressed to my head. But I liked it that way. I was going to die trying. Exactly what a good son would do.

Chapter 23

ON THE FIRST TURN, on the inside of the track, I hit the tacky clay. Giorgio's rear tire bit into it perfectly. He'd had the crew stagger the tires just right. I flew past number 27, Tommy Mulligan, nearly clipping his car.

Only thirteen drivers to beat. The only way to do this was one at a time.

I clutched the wing lever for dear life.

Number 45, Kyle Goodard, was dead ahead.

I rode his tire tracks into the second turn. My back wheel swung around, over-rotating, but instinct kicked in. A skilled pull of the lever tightened the car to perfection. I saw my chance!

I throttled Goldilock's 360-cubic-inch V-8 so hard it screamed, as I charged out of the corner and blew past Goodard! "Fucking-A, Randy!" I shouted. He'd perfectly matched the tire pressure to the track temperature and maxed-out the spring rate. "If you ain't got the spring, you ain't got the swing, baby! God-*damn!*"

I revelled in the beautiful beast I was driving tonight. Giorgio's car fit me like a glove, like my old mini stock. It was like a big, roaring extension of my body.

All of our crates on the track were *hot*, sliding, veering, and pinching. The sound of zipping, thundering cars supercharged me, just the way it used to.

Thirty-four more laps. You can do this!

But the next corner was a disaster. I hammered in too tight and slid in deep. Goodard jacked past me, and so did the Iron Man and Dougie Pounder.

I swore a blue streak and tore after them recklessly. But anger and speed are a bad mix, as I knew, of course. I clipped car 94's front end and sent it into a dangerous side slide. My crate went into a terrible wobble and I had to fight the judder in my steering wheel.

My heart was pounding a crazy bongo beat. Eventually I righted the car and started breathing again. I sent up a prayer of thanks that I hadn't crashed, that no one had crashed. Soggy dirt coated my tongue.

Dicing with Giorgio hadn't prepared me for this. Not even close. This race was the most jittery, crazy contest I'd ever driven.

For the next four laps, I ran out of racing room. The pressure to win was excruciating. My bladder just about burst.

On lap twenty-nine, I drove deep into the third corner, got some serious tire bite and smoked past four cars. Fucking-A I did!

Car 81 blew a tire and hobbled off the track. One less car to beat!

By the thirty-first lap, I'd grappled my way into sixth place. Between the heat from the engine and nervous concentration, I was swimming in sweat.

Next on deck was two-time Canadian Nationals champ Jake Hennessy. He ran a tight race and was a real pro in the corners. But when we hit the third corner, I found a full head of steam and blew past him down to the inside. Holy shit! Even *I* was impressed with my driving.

A pack of drivers was fighting for third—Clay Farley, number 9, Josh Torrance, number 16, and Billy Dunn, number 42. Clay had won the Nationals last year, beating out Giorgio. And Josh and Billy had a handful of seconds and thirds under their belts and were hot for first. These guys were all gods on the track.

On the back straight, I pinched past Billy and Clay. I swung in behind Josh, but every time I tried to pass, he cut me off. Every time Billy and Clay tried to pass me, I cut *them* off.

I hit the turn shallow and blew past Josh. I felt like I was dreaming. But I'd done it! *Again!* I was now in third place! I hammer-fisted the steering wheel. "Suck on that, Beppe!" I roared, and then I hacked, with a lungful of dust.

I held third place until the thirty-third lap.

On the third turn, I went in too fast and missed the wall by inches.

When my heart started beating again, the tailing drivers had soared past.

Oh man, I'd forgotten how scary it was to almost die. It was a good reminder to use my damn head. I made a small lever adjustment, cranked the throttle, and reclaimed third.

All I had to do now was pass two cars and win.

On Lap thirty-four Tanner Hunt was in second. Last year's fifth place finisher, Antron Lynch, number 63, was in first.

On the second turn, I hit the outside of the track too fast. In a textbook slide, my rear end swung around hard. I slowed a smidge and the car righted.

But my miscalculation had been just the ticket for Billy and Josh to pass—again!

"Fuck! Fuck! Fuck! Fuck! Fuck!"

Preparation! Teamwork! Focus! I repeated Luke's mantra as I caught up and glued myself to Josh and Billy.

Third turn.

C'mon, Tony! *Win or die trying!*

I got a good run off the corner and hit the inside, but Josh misjudged the turn. I rocketed past him!

I swung to track bottom and ran fast and steady. Before the next turn, I hunted Billy half-way up the corner, shot past and tracked bottom again. I was back in third position!

Then the white flag dropped.

One lap to go! One lap to get it done.

But then horrible dread pissed through my body. It hit me that I *wasn't* going to win—Tanner and Antron were too far ahead.

Tears streamed down my face, almost blinding me. I'd failed Ma, Giorgio, my family. It was over. All was lost.

Then, for some stupid fucking reason, I realized that deep, deep down, I'd wanted to win so my old man would be proud of me. Just like poor Giorgio. Now I really wanted to kill myself.

I swung out of the final turn and crossed the finish line, far behind Tanner and Antron. After some cool down laps, I drove towards my pit.

A crowd was waiting there.

Chapter 24

AS I HAULED MYSELF out of the car, I was swarmed by cheering friends and family.

What the fuck? Had they missed the part where I came in far behind the first and second place cars?

"Third place!" Ma cried, tears streaming down her face. "I'm so proud of you, son!" She hugged me up, her arms still surprisingly strong after all these years.

"Ma," I said, gently pulling away. "I'm so sorry." But Ma's face still beamed. Had she forgotten the part where she and Dad just lost everything?

"Awesome job, Tony," Donny said, clapping me on the back.

"You were incredible!" Norb wheezed.

John smiled his pearly whites.

I gazed around the big circle of well-wishers, still in shock.

Everyone from the Village was there, from the cashier at the Village Variety to the stock boy from Price Chopper. Even Father Carlo was there, sporting gold face paint.

At the edges, curious fans.

Including Tanner.

I beckoned to Angie to come closer. I really needed her arms around me right now.

A CHCH TV reporter shoved a mic in my face and faced her camera man. "This is Jan Harley reporting from Hermonville Raceway. Today, we're talking to Tony the Prodigy Valentini. Back in the early eighties, the Prodigy won seven consecutive racing titles, a record that still stands." She beamed at me. "Tony how does it feel to have made the greatest comeback in Hermonville racing history?"

"Comeback? Look, I came third. The winner here tonight was Tanner Hunt."

"Oh, I think your fans would beg to differ." She held out the microphone and the circle of people around us went nuts.

The outpouring of support was just too much. My face crumpled and I pawed away my tears.

Jan Harley turned back to me. "To come out of retirement after twenty years and place third in the Canadian Sprint Car Nationals is unprecedented! How were you able to achieve such a remarkable feat?"

How? Extortion, threats against the people I loved, that kind of thing, Jan. Yeah, that would have been some answer.

"Thanks for coming everyone," I said bluntly, turning away and cutting through the crowd. I had to get out of there—there was nothing good to say about this nightmare.

The crowd parted for me like the Red Sea.

Dad stood there in front of me. For once he didn't look away like a guilty dog. He was laser-focussed on me. He had something to say, I could tell. But I'd beat him to it. I'd out him, so everyone there would know what a piece of shit he was. It would be one hell of a broadcast tonight at old CHCH!

The group around me stopped talking. I opened my mouth to rip into Dad, but he raised a silencing hand and I instinctively shut my mouth. Like I was his little boy again. Spellbound by my hero.

He took a careful step toward me. His voice was calm, but there was a tiny tremor in his hands. "Tony, there was no debt."

There was a roaring in my ears, even though everyone around me was stunned into silence.

"Wh-what?" I stammered. "No debt?" I blurted. My brain seemed to have stopped processing. "What the hell are you talking about?"

Beppe and his cronies shoved through the crowd. He smiled sweetly at me. "Tony, what your papa said is true." Gone was his mafia schtick. "There never was a gambling debt. He made it up so you'd race again, and everyone you love played their part to make sure that happened."

My father shifted on his feet, glancing at Ma, who gave him a little nod of encouragement.

"I always felt so bad I was the reason you quit. So, I devised a plan to get you back doing what you were born to do." His voice dropped to almost a whisper. "That's how much I love you."

"His lie was a kind of gift to you," Beppe added.

Toto whipped out the same gun he'd brandished at me in the Windstar. "Fake," he grinned. He held it up for everyone to see. It really was fake!

"Bullshit!" I barked at Beppe, fighting to keep my grip on reality. "What kind of idiot do you think I am?" Heaving, burning emotions ran havoc inside me. "You're a liar!" I raged at Dad. "Just like this sack of shit mobster!"

My mother gave a little gasp and clutched my arm. "Tony!" she chided. I ripped my arm away, raging.

But Dad was nodding. Was he *agreeing* he was a liar? What a liar move!

I searched my mother's face, hoping she'd confirm that Dad and Beppe were still lying. But she gave me a look, knowing and apologetic.

What the hell was happening? Reality had left the raceway. I felt Angie slip her hand in mine, anchoring me.

The tension was brutal.

"Hey, Tony, come on," Toto cajoled me. "Can we act or what? As good as DeNiro and Pacino in *The Godfather*, right?" He winked at Doughboy. "Beppe would have made a great Vito Corleone," he continued. I glared at him, and he shrugged dramatically. "What, am I wrong?" He straightened the lapel of his sports coat. A goofy smile softened his face.

Beppe raised his hands towards me. "As the Bard said: 'This above all: to thine own self be true, And it must follow, as the night the day, Thou canst not then be false to any man.'"

"Hamlet," Allison cried. "Polonius's speech. Well done, Beppe!"

"Well, I'll be hog-tied!" Donny cried.

Beppe bowed to his captive audience.

Frickin' Shakespeare? Ma pressed her hand against my chest and gazed up at me. "Your Papa loves you, Tony. Sure, he's a loser, and he's lost too many times to count, and, yes, he disappointed you and your sister so much, but he always wanted the best for you."

Dad's lips were in a tight, thin line.

He'd convinced everyone to pretend because he *loved* me?

I choked up. "You acted, too, Ma?"

She nodded. "Everyone did, son."

"Angie?" I looked at her in disbelief. Had my wife been lying to me, too?

Angie looked regretful. "Tone, don't be mad, OK? This whole thing was intended to help you, alright? Like—like an intervention."

John squeezed my shoulder. "Look, Tony, we all knew you shouldn't have quit. You were born to race. You're the Prodigy, buddy. So everyone acted their part to get you back on the track."

Angie took both my hands in hers. "Think about it, honey. Haven't you felt more alive, more like the old you, since you got back behind the wheel?"

I was trying to understand how everyone I knew *lying* to me and putting me through *hell* was *helpful*, when Giorgio popped out of the crowd. He'd changed out of his racing suit.

"Giorgio?" I cried. "Where the hell were you?"

He didn't respond. His eyes were fixed on Beppe.

Beppe slung a loving arm over his son's shoulders. "Tony," he said, "some things that happened *are* true. But before I speak further, I want to apologize for scaring you when you were little. We had no right showing up at your house dressed like cold-blooded killers. Seeing us like that must have terrified you. And for that I am truly sorry."

Toto nodded, looking regretful.

Is this really happening?

"I'm also sorry for turning your Papa into an absentee father," Beppe said. "I should have helped him with his addiction, instead of making it worse." Ma nodded at him sternly, and Beppe gave Dad a penitent look. "I'm truly sorry, Frank."

But Dad wasn't looking at Beppe. His eyes were still glued to me. Ma squeezed him close.

The crowd was totally spellbound. And I was totally mind-fucked.

"But I'm not a monster, Tony," Beppe continued, guiltily. "I let your Dad pay off his debt to me by working for me. It took him ten years, but he did pay it back, *all* of it."

Numbness spread through my chest and down my forearms. "So, let me see if I've got everything straight. Everyone I know play-acted to get me back behind the wheel?" My voice cracked. "My parents lied to me about Dad owing four-hundred grand? And Giorgio bailed on me so I'd be forced to drive his car? Just to prove to myself that I'd thrown away my talent?"

"This was all my idea," Dad said. "Don't blame your mother."

Ma locked her gaze on me. "Don't be mad, Tony. Your father wanted you to realize that you can still have your dream."

My emotions were a shocked, gooey mess. *Was* I mad? I wasn't sure exactly what I was feeling, but it wasn't great, that's for sure.

Hot tears stung my eyes. I was beginning to feel like a real piece of shit for the way I'd treated my Dad, and for so long, too.

"I'm the only professional actor," Beppe offered. "I'm a regular at Theatre Aquarius."

"He's really good," Ma murmured. "Your Dad and I have seen all his plays."

Some of the people near me nodded. Apparently, they had too.

Beppe bowed dramatically. A frickin' *actor?* That was almost worse.

Desperate to anchor myself, to make sure what I'd heard was true, I said, "And everyone was definitely in on it?" I searched the Villager's faces. "What the hell? Like *The Sting?*"

I turned to my friends. "Donny? That fits." I shook my head. "But Norb? *John?* How could you guys?"

Donny just shrugged at me, grinning a little. Norb's face went into a spasm of guilt, and he made an apologetic little squeak.

John looked at me soberly. "It was kind of a shitty trick, we know. But you needed it, Tony. You've looked after everybody else for years. Just denying yourself the chance to really live. You've been there for us, time after time. We agreed to go along with this crazy scheme to be there for *you*, as nutty as that sounds."

"Sorry, Tony," Norb sighed. "Sorry we lied to you."

I didn't want to think too much about how my wife had deceived me, so I focussed back on the crowd of neighbours from the Village. How had they coordinated this massive effort?

I glanced at my father, who wouldn't look at me.

Beppe cleared his throat. "We have something else to tell you, Tony," he said.

Everyone pressed in closer, but I noticed my mother seemed to shrink back a little.

"You've got to be kidding," I said. How much more was I supposed to take?

He looked grim. "You gotta take what I'm gonna tell you like a man. Right? Cause this is big."

Out of the corner of my eye, I saw Dad take Ma's hand.

"Your pops worked for me because he owed a lot more than money. When—"

"Papa!" Giorgio broke in. "Please, this is too hard for you. Let me tell Tony. It's my story to tell."

Beppe and Giorgio threw their arms around each other, and the old charlatan said, "I love you, Giorgio."

"I love you, too." Their voices were muffled by their bearhug.

Some of the crowd actually *awwed*.

Then Giorgio faced me. He spoke slowly and carefully, with great sensitivity. "I don't know if you're aware of this, but I have a sister, Isabella. She's a lot older than me. Nineteen years older. The thing is, last year she and Papa told me she's not really my sister. She's my mother."

The people around me gasped. Well, that was a bombshell. I was wondering where Giorgio was going with this.

Giorgio continued, looking almost excited. "Papa raised me and Isabella all on his own, and he was a great father. So he was very upset that this young man got his daughter pregnant, so he made that man, my father, work for him. All his earnings were to go back to Beppe to help support me and Isabella." Giorgio nodded at me, encouraging me to understand. But I just stared, my stupid brain like a block of ice.

"The man who is my father already had a family. So now he had two families to support, two jobs to work. He did his best, but it meant he couldn't be with either family as much as he wanted."

OK. The truth was starting to seep into the edges of my brain.

"Tony," Giorgio beamed, "my dad is Frank Valentini!"

I felt like I'd just taken a baseball bat to the face.

"Don't you see, Tony?" Giorgio cried, slapping his hands against his face. "We're half- brothers. Isn't that marvelous?"

Shock tingled through my arms and legs like electric snakes. This revelation felt *cruel*. Now I hated Dad more than ever!

My brain heaved and grinded as I tried to absorb just a single atom of this life-altering fuckery. I turned to my mother. Her eyes were red, and she looked stricken, but she met my gaze and nodded slowly. That asshole! My poor ma!

Giorgio continued earnestly, "I didn't know, not until Papa told me last year. Frank was always so nice to me, taking me places, talking about the stuff I liked. So when I found out he was my birth dad, I wasn't too upset. Papa did a real good job raising me, so I couldn't be mad at him for keeping a secret. And then I found out Frank had other kids!" He pounded his heart, choking up. "I'm just so glad I've finally met my brother. I've been dreaming of this day for almost a year. I'm sorry I didn't tell you earlier, Tony. It just wasn't the right time."

"You're my half-brother?" I whispered. Everything was blurry and slow now. I felt Angie squeeze my arm reassuringly.

"Oh," Giorgio added, excitedly, "and Elio is also kind of my stepbrother. Papa had a one-night stand with Elio's mum, Miss Cherry. She's a professional dancer. Anyway, that kinda makes him *your* quarter brother."

"Oh," I managed to say, completely dazed. Doughboy gave me a stupid grin. *I don't think so.* I thanked God we weren't blood-related.

I realized that I had been slowly backing up, searching for an escape route through the crowd. But the ring of people tightened.

I looked to Angie for strength, and her smile gave me a much-needed blast of Team Tony. It was just what I needed to keep from losing my mind.

Giorgio's eyes were locked on me, searching for my approval. The pained look on his face made me realize how hard it must have been for him, not being able to meet me. *Shit!* He was one more person I had to look after now. One more person I'd probably let down! I reminded myself that he was grown-up. And I was only his half-brother. *Not* his father. No, *that* guy was Frank Valentini.

Now that I knew Dad's full story—his lying and philandering—on top of this fraud he'd played on me, I was pretty sure I could *never* forgive him. He and Ma were hanging onto each other for dear life now, fighting to keep each other from falling. I noticed the greying hair, the deep lines in their faces. Had my lack of forgiveness done this—prematurely aged them?

A swell of rage energized me. No, my father had screwed Beppe's daughter! He'd betrayed *my* mother, and then she'd had to spend the rest of her life sharing him and keeping his dirty secret! That was unforgiveable!

Ma was still looking at Dad. She had so much love in her eyes, it was shocking. But I felt disgust. It made her look weak. *Didn't it?*

Her words rang in my ears. *Take it like a man.*

Between Giorgio and Ma, my resolve to never forgive Dad was weakening. My heart spun with so many versions of right and wrong I couldn't keep track.

I told myself that, if Giorgio could forgive *our* dad and even Beppe could forgive him, then a resentful, prideful guy like me could, maybe. If I was being honest with myself, I was sick to death of holding a grudge. It was exhausting. It was juvenile. And what had it ever done for me? Fill me with misery and pain, that's what.

I realized in all this hub bub that my Dad had said almost nothing. I was relieved because it gave me the chance to understand how my feelings for him were changing.

Shit on a stick! I realized I was going to have to forgive my dad. There was no other way through this mess. *Fake it till you make it*, I grumbled at myself.

I told myself that, although Dad was an adulterous asshole and a deadbeat dad, he'd also given life to an amazing human being, gifting me with a super-nice brother, which would be pretty cool—once I got over all the mindfuckery. I offered Dad a curt nod.

Angel caught the play and ran up and hugged me. "He's so nice, Dad," Angel said. "I really like him."

"Can I call you Uncle Giorgio?" Angel asked, shyly, smiling up at him.

"Golly," Giorgio said, "that would be the best!" He gave my daughter a high-five and grinned at me, thrilled.

"This is so unreal," I mumbled to myself.

"I know it is," Angie said, rubbing my back. "But you'll get used to it. You'll see. I'll help you." She buried her face in my chest.

I locked eyes with my father. We looked so much alike. I was a chunkier version of him, but we were both stubborn to a fault. And I'd always been so proud of myself for not being like him.

But now, the hurt in his eyes mirrored the hurt in my heart. And I felt an uncontrollable pang that things had been so rotten between us for so long. So much pride and anger on my part. So much shame and addiction on his. What a waste.

I wiped the tears stinging my eyes. Ma's words from the other day rolled through my head, "I just want my family back. You, Josie, your papa, and me. I want us to be a family again. Before I die. That's all I care about."

For the first time in years, I really *saw* my dad. Another wave of guilt struck me. Even after all his mistakes, Dad deserved better. He'd put a roof over my head. He'd fed me. He'd loved Ma. Those counted for something. I gave him a tiny nod to show him I was willing to try to forgive. Half of the estrangement had been my fault. I recognized that now.

"So, um, there's just one more thing," Giorgio laughed nervously. "It's a real doozy."

"No," I groaned. "Dear God, are you trying to kill me?" But I gave him my attention. After all, he was my brother.

The crowd pressed in eagerly.

"Don't worry, Tony. This isn't about you. It's about me." Giorgio faced Beppe. He was just about vibrating with tensions.

Not about me? First good news in this whole bizarre mess!

"Papa, you need to know the real reason I never won a race. Why I always came second."

Laughing uneasily, Beppe surveyed his audience. Gesturing with his stogie, he said. "Because you were anxious you'd lose, right?"

"Partially," Giorgio said. "But mostly because I was afraid to *win*."

Beppe looked like he'd been smacked in the face with a big fish. "Afraid to *win*? What are you talking about? *Everybody* wants to win!"

Giorgio shook his head. "Dr. Hotz said maybe I was scared to be the person I wasn't meant to be."

The crowd was rapt. They'd certainly gotten their money's worth today.

"Pappa, the only reason I raced was to make you happy. I wanted you to be proud of me. But as I got older, I realized I'd been living a lie."

Beppe's face went white. He swallowed and steeled himself for his son to come out of the closet. It was practically in a thought bubble over his head.

Giorgio gasped. "I'm joining the seminary! I'm going to be a priest!"

"A priest?" A flash of anger crossed Beppe's face. "Are you crazy? What kind of job is *that*? What do they have to do all day? Listen to malefactors like me, with their list of sins for the confessional! Then they have to say, 'Your sins are forgiven. Go in peace.' Forgiven! It must give them heartburn!"

"I've made up my mind, Papa. I knew from the time I was a little boy I wanted to be a priest. I've always known."

Beppe smacked his forehead with his hand. "I knew I shouldn't have hired Sister Maria to homeschool you. A priest? *Dio mio!*"

Giorgio just looked determined.

Beppe gulped a deep breath and slowly exhaled, studying his son. He smiled weakly. "I love you, Giorgio. I always knew you were different and that's okay. I really didn't expect this, but I want you to be happy, son. That's everything to me." He pulled Giorgio into a hug.

This was no acting.

Beppe, his face wet with tears, pointed at me. His voice was strong and assured. "Tony Valentini, unlike Giorgio Santucci, *you* were born to race! And if you don't take hold of your destiny with both hands, you are a fool."

Giorgio pulled away and clapped me on the shoulders, and I suddenly realized something.

Holy shit! We both have Dad's nose!

"Brother!" he cried, "behind you! Quick!"

Past the cameraman still filming us—I'd had no fight left to tell him or the reporter to hit the road—Tanner drove up in a brand new, candy apple red sprint car. He parked it in front of me.

He slid out of the open cockpit and motioned me towards it.

"What's this?" I asked.

"It's yours," Giorgio said.

"What?"

Angela spoke up. "You deserve it, Tony. You were born to race. I know it, your dad knows it, our kids know it, everyone knows it. Just go ahead," she said gently. "Give it a spin."

"Everyone bought it for you, Dad," Angel cried, tearing up. "It was Nonno's idea. *Pleeeze,* Dad!"

Everyone had...*bought* me a sprint car?

"You belong here," Angie said. "You always did. No more excuses, okay?" She stood on her tip toes and whispered in my ear. "And no more sadness."

"Was I that obvious?" I said, my voice cracking. So much for my years of manly stoicism.

Snuffling, she buried her face in my chest.

Dad had eyes on me. I offered him a weak smile. He really had helped do a wonderful thing for me. I gave him a thumbs up to thank him, but I couldn't speak to him   the little boy inside me was bawling. And it was in that difficult moment that I knew I'd stepped onto the road of true forgiveness.

Pulled by a supernatural force, I found myself climbing into the sprint car. Oh, it was a beauty.

My friends and family gathered around, smiling, daubing tears.

Moved by their show of love, lightning-bolted by gratitude, I sobbed like a little boy, decades of stress and hurt finally emptying out of me.

Chapter 25

THE NEXT DAY.

Norb had showed up during my lunch break, carrying a bag of my favourite comfort foods—a walnut crunch donut, a meatball sub, and an extra-large black coffee. For himself, he'd brought a torpedo sub with real bacon and a chocolate milk. Like always, we sat on the edge of the concrete planter across from the service bay and chowed down.

We'd been discussing the Hermonville insanity when Norb let it slip that he'd seen Walker filming us there. "Norb, you idiot!" he shouted at himself. He'd driven his meaty palm against his forehead. "You said you wouldn't say anything!"

"It's okay, buddy," I'd said, anger burning a hole through my chest. "You were born honest. That's a good thing. So, what happened? Last I saw, you guys and that weird impersonator were heading to Walker's place. I thought you were going to keep him busy?"

Norb's face went fire-engine red. "We'd tried, but when we got there, that butthead had left us a note on the door saying, 'Nice try losers. See you at the Raceway.'"

He shook his head and dug into his sub.

Although I'd tried to keep cool for Norb's sake, I wolfed down my sub and found myself angrily pacing a groove in the pavement. Determined to end Walker's stalking once and for all, I called Donny, telling him and John to meet Norb and me at Walker's house in twenty minutes.

I was having some pretty violent fantasies. I was going to bust down his door, hogtie him, and get Donny to take photos. I'd tell him I was going to post his face all over town, on flyers announcing he was a serial killer. And then I'd root out every last strip of film he'd ever taken of us and burn it in a bonfire in his backyard—and make the fucker watch! I'd tape his eyelids open, if I had to!

All hepped up at the thought, I bounced on my toes and curled my fists.

Norb was terrified of me. He was right to be. I was out for blood.

I ran toward my van. "C'mon, Norb! Time to whup some ass!"

Clutching the last bite of his sub, Norb booted after me.

He'd barely closed his door when I was burning rubber out onto Flux Road. The tires squealed as I tore around the traffic circle at the top of the Kenilworth Access. Norb clutched the dashboard and squeezed his eyes shut as we barreled down the road toward the north end.

Under his breath, he was singing "Say a Little Prayer", and I got the distinct impression that he'd turned it into an *actual* prayer, because he reached over and squeezed my hand. In one of the weirdest situations of the past few days (and that was really saying something), I found myself joining in. I had a terrible voice and I got most of the lyrics wrong, but still.

It should have been weird praying with The Steeltown Avenger. Instead, it was comforting. Besides, with what I had planned for Dave Walker, I needed every prayer I could get.

Because I'd probably go to Hell for what I was going to do.

Chapter 26

THE HOPE AND STRENGTH I'd gathered, knowing the Steeltown Avenger was beside me, vanished when his hand slipped out of mine. Norb was beefed out in his seat, snoring like a baby. Stress had done a number on him, so he'd checked out, in classic Norb style.

But at least the Screw had been straight up about his intentions, I thought. Walker, on the other hand, hadn't. Who knew what he really wanted? Tracking down and filming a bunch of former high school nobodies? What kind of person does that? And why?

I had no idea if I was being courageous or stupid or both. Being a vigilante was dangerous and lawless, I knew that. And I'd spent my entire life being a responsible citizen. But for the sake of my friends and their families, it was up to me to stop Walker. I couldn't see it any other way.

I was way past giving a shit about his reasons for his bizarre behaviour. All I cared about was shutting the psycho down before he drove *me* totally fucking insane, too!

I'd always thought of my brain as a BRM engine, and knowing I was going to confront Walker had all sixteen cylinders firing beautifully.

Behind me stretched a line of angry, honking drivers. Apparently, my sprint racing skills were not appreciated on the streets of the Hammer.

I kept replaying the events at the Raceway, cringing as I remembered all the deeply personal reveals. And how fucked up I'd felt later on at home, watching my CHCH TV interview. Hearing the reporter call me "the Prodigy" had made me feel like a retarded adolescent. "I've grown up, dammit!" I'd yelled at the TV. "Get that into your head once and for all!"

When I caught my reflection in the bathroom mirror this morning, I was shocked. A total burnout stared back, looking twenty years older.

I was the ugly guy from *The Good, The Bad and The Ugly*—if he'd gone on a three-week bender. What the frig did Angie see in me? Between my raging temper and my bulldog face, I was definitely no prize!

I hammered the dashboard. *Stop beating yourself up! Listen, you won a 15-lap and placed third in the frickin' Special, ya big baby! You're not so bad! Just focus!* I took the tight corner at the bottom of the access too fast, tilting the van hard. The screeching tires startled Norb awake. He clamped his paws against his face, wheezing in terror.

"Hang in there, buddy," I said, patting his shoulder, as we thumped back down onto all four wheels. "Remember, I'm a professional, OK? I'm not going to crash us."

Norb looked embarrassed.

I found my mind wandering to worst case scenarios because of my dark mood. What if Walker sold the footage of us to a news channel and it went viral the way Donny's columns had? Would Donny then turn *my* story into a movie? He'd probably hire Maurice to play me, damn him! What would he call it? *Need For Speed: The Tony Valentini Story?* Actually, I kinda liked that title. Steven Dundee would be a better choice to play me, but Patricia would have to strap a prosthetic gut on him.

What the hell was I doing? Dammit! Donny had infected me with his stupid disease! I pounded the dashboard again.

Norb screeched, the highest, shrillest peep ever, breaking his old record by at least a hundred decibels! I expected to see every dog in Hamilton coming running after us.

"Sorry, Norb," I said. "I didn't mean to scare you." I reached out to pat his arm and he flinched away, giving me the side-eye.

Now I felt like a complete shit. "Norb, you know I'd *never* hurt you." *Tony, get it together, man. You're acting like a jerk.*

I tried one more time, slowly reaching over and rubbing Norb's shoulder. He suddenly went calm, like a crated dog.

As I sped north on Kenilworth, I found that Dad was renting space in my head. Last week, while I'd bawled my eyes out inside my new sprint car, Dad and Ma had quietly waited for me. Elio and Beppe and Toto had put the run on everyone to give us some private family time, but I'd wished they hadn't. I'd needed some more time to process everything. And there was a *lot* of different issues in that 'everything'.

As I'd climbed out of the sprint car, I'd offered Dad a weak smile, and he'd given one back. But that was all I had.

Ma had said nothing. She'd seemed content we were finally acknowledging each other.

Baby steps, I'd thought. Angie's advice was always solid.

Isabella, Giorgio's mom, had been nineteen when Dad had knocked her up. It sickened me to know he'd done it with a teenager, but at least she'd been of legal age.

I snorted. So Isabella was my half-brother's mom. Did that mean we were sort of related?

And what about Ma? Either she was a sad case, a door mat—or she was capable of a kind of deep, forgiving love that I couldn't imagine myself giving. Obviously, my mother had never been a door mat, but I didn't believe Dad deserved her forgiveness. I grudgingly admitted to myself that giving it where it hasn't been earned might be the point of forgiveness.

Something else that was really hard to swallow was, well...everything that had happened, beginning with Doughboy throwing sand in Angel's gas tank. Had everyone I knew really been play-acting to get me to race? Lying, really. Repeatedly.

Angie had lied, too, even when she saw what a basket case the whole charade was making me. I wanted to be furious, but I couldn't get there.

And my friends? Well, after all the bizarre shit we'd been through together in the past couple of years, this scheme did kinda track.

Miraculously, they hadn't fucked up their parts, not even Donny. Hard to frickin' believe.

And all of this had been Dad's idea because he *loved* me. My dad loved me.

All this thinking about love should have softened me up, right? Should have made me turn the car around, swear off violence, sing Kum Ba Yah around the campfire?

It didn't.

I went back to salivating over the evil I was going to do to Walker.

Chapter 27

WALKER'S BUNGALOW WAS on Burlington Street, across the road from Dofasco. Like the other homes crowded into the block, it was tired and grimy with dust. A truck loaded up with ingots heaved through the factory gates.

Norb was leaning against front of the van, biting his thumb, nervously scanning for Donny and John. "I should have worn my body armour," he muttered to himself. "And the cape. And the mask."

I was feeling guilty for dragging him to this showdown. It was going to involve breaking the law—amongst other things. Despite his Steeltown Avenger schtick, Norb didn't have a mean bone in his body. "Listen, you don't have to be a part of this, Norb," I said.

He looked offended. "How can you say that? We're a team—all four of us! Of course I'm in!" He stood straight up, trying to look tough.

John skidded his car to the curb.

When Donny got out, I raged at him, "Love, you hero-worshipping asshole! This is all your fault!"

John looked at me in alarm, but Donny wasn't fazed.

"Let's do this, mother-fuckers!" he cried. "Let's finish Walker, once and for all!"

And there was Love in a nutshell. One minute self-absorbed and infuriating. The next minute, when the chips were down, he was one for all, all for one. And somehow, since he'd returned to The Hammer, it was like he'd never left. How the fuck did he do that?

He ran past me and led the charge.

"No you don't!" I shoved past him and practically leapt up the concrete steps and pounded on the front door. Donny added an extra pounding for good measure, grinning at me.

"His car's not here," John said, coming up the steps with Norb. "Maybe he's not home." He sounded hopeful.

"He's home," Donny insisted, "I'm sure of it."

"You don't know that," I griped. I really didn't want to lose my steam on this.

"Think about it, Tony," Donny said. "Walker gets off on filming us. He needs it! Filming us while we break into his house would give him a massive hard-on."

"No one wants to see that," John muttered.

"No one films me or my family," I barked, pounding again.

"Wait!" Donny said, his hand pressed against the brick wall.

"What?"

"House is cold."

"So?"

"So, I was wrong. He's not home."

"Bullshit. I bet he's hiding in the closet right now."

"I'm telling you, when Walker's home, the brick's warm. The house is alive."

"Woah," said Norb, lighting up, "like *The Haunting of Hill House*."

"You got it, Norbster."

John and I just shook our heads at each other.

I was about to kick the door down when Donny lunged at me and gripped me by the collars. His face was manic. "I know a better way, brother. Trust me. It's almost finished."

I ripped his hands off me.

"What's almost finished, Donny?" Norb asked, innocent as a lamb.

"My tunnel."

We all stared at him. Jesus, Mary, and Joseph! What had he done now?

"I built it in Walker's back yard. It's taken me two years."

This little nugget of news just about pickled my brain. And I knew that look on his face all too well—he was totally telling the truth.

Were we in some kind of horror movie? It was like we were getting ready to face Freddy Kruger, only to discover that Jason Voorhees was standing beside me, readying the 'ol chainsaw to help us out.

Donny was trembling with excitement. "Shovel and enter. Easy in, easy out! Together we shall vanquish Walker. Onward, ho!"

Donny sailed off the porch and we ran in behind him. We couldn't stop ourselves.

"Two frickin' years. He's been tunnelling under Dave Walker's yard, like a psychotic mole, for two frickin years?" John said under his breath.

Oh yeah, I was pretty sure Donny had crossed over into real insanity.

I was terrified for him. For all of us. This was all so way beyond the pale, as Archie Love was always saying. The only good part was that Donny's extreme craziness had stopped my rage in its tracks. I didn't want to beat Walker anymore. At least, I was pretty sure I didn't. I definitely didn't want any of us to go to jail, but it was looking more and more likely we would.

I don't know you, Donny, I thought, *I've never really known you.*

Poor Norb was back to singing his Burt Bacharach prayer.

At the side of the house, Donny unhitched a tall wooden gate, and in we all went. A six-foot privacy fence surrounded a backyard the size of a postage stamp.

Holy shit!

Towering at least nine feet tall, a marble statue of young Steven Dundee wailed into a microphone, frozen in time. He'd been transformed into some kind of alabaster god.

"Woah," Norb breathed. "So beautiful."

In a museum, the statue would have been friggin' art, but not here in a shitty backyard in a shitty part of town, filthy with factory smoke and reeking of sulphur.

"Did you do this?" I asked Donny accusingly. "What—? What the hell?"

"It's...amazing," John said.

Donny turned back towards the statue. "I wanted to tell you guys earlier but I thought it would be too much, what with everything else going on. I'm thinking Walker had it made. It was here when I arrived to dig the tunnel. I had nothing to do with it."

Norb had edged closer and was gaping at Our Dear Lord Steven, his hand resting on the marble Converse sneaker.

"Who gives a fuck about the statue!" I snapped. "Get us inside now, Love, or we're aborting the mission!"

"Roger that!"

We followed him to the center of the lawn, where the statue stood on a huge concrete pad.

Donny tore back a flap of sod, then whipped a flashlight out of his coat and shone light into the dark hole. Cursing myself for getting sucked into yet another Donny Love scheme, I followed him down into the tunnel. Norb's prayer song got louder as he and John brought up the rear. Except for Donny's light, it was now pitch black.

"Wouldn't it have been be easier to just break the lock on the back door?" John griped. "And we're going to get filthy down here."

"Do you think there are spiders?" Norb sounded pretty anxious.

Personally, I was more concerned with whether there was *oxygen* down there.

The tunnel was the height of a crawlspace, and about a yard wide, framed in two-by-fours.

"Anyone else feeling a bit claustrophobic?" John asked, as we crawled along on our hands and knees.

The smell was damp and earthy. Dirt dug under my nails. Cold, sharp stones scraped my palms. My arthritic knee was barking.

"You dug this all by yourself?" I panted.

"Yep," Donny said.

"You're fucked up, Donny," I said. "Sorry, man, but that's the truth."

Donny made a non-committal sound.

John and Norb were quiet behind me, probably terrified the tunnel was going to collapse or a giant spider was lying in wait. Personally, I was worried that Walker was waiting for us up ahead, swinging an axe.

Sweat stung my eyes. The sense that we would be buried alive was going ape shit on me. I was about to scream at Donny to get us the fuck out of there when Norb suddenly stopped. John's head struck his butt, and they both let out a yelp.

We'd been dead-ended by the house's cinder block foundation. Donny had left a fourteen-pound hammer leaning against it.

"Strike while the iron's hot!" Donny cried. He tried to grab the hammer, but I beat him to it.

The guys dove out of the way as I wound up and swung from the side. All my rage and fear powered through me. The hammer easily blew a hole through the cinder block.

"Holy cow!" Norb cried. "Tony, you've got super powers!"

Eight more swings and I'd smashed a jagged hole big enough for four grown-ass idiots to crawl through.

"Break on through to the other side!" Donny sang.

"Keep it down, Jim Morrison," I hissed. Of course, the pounding of the sledgehammer would have wakened the dead, so it really didn't matter. I was just being cranky.

"What if he's home now?" Norb whispered, nervously rubbing his cheek. "What if he calls the police on us?"

At this point, I barely gave a shit. I was just so glad to get out of that damn tunnel. We crawled over the rubble into the basement.

John used his phone flashlight to locate a bare light bulb hanging from the ceiling.

In the dim yellow light, we could see that the wall beyond the stairs had split down the middle, as if something evil was pressing against it from the other side.

A small runner of water trickled down to the floor and into a cob-webbed drain. In a shadowy corner, a rusted boiler made horrible groaning sounds. The reek of mildew was so bad it was making us gag.

Donny told us to remove our shoes so we wouldn't track mud. We brushed it off our clothes as best we could and tip-toed along the cold concrete floor and up the creaking stairs. They were worn and oil-stained. The door at the top was closed. My heart was thumping. Was Walker on the other side, waiting to dismember us? Considering everything that had happened in the past few weeks, it really wasn't that much of a stretch.

The guys looked as messed up as I felt. They'd moved to one side so I'd be the one to open the door. We all knew this was my idea, so that was fair.

I tried the door handle, but it wouldn't budge. I jiggled it so hard it busted apart in my hand.

Preparing myself for the worst, I kicked the door open, threw up my meat hooks, and charged into the living room, yelling like a berserker. The boys tumbled in behind me, hollering chaotically.

Walker was not wielding a chainsaw, or a camera. In fact, he was nowhere to be seen.

Chapter 28

BEFORE FINALLY CRASHING on Walker's living room couch, we'd scoured every nook and cranny to make sure he wasn't hiding. We'd checked for hidden cameras but had come up empty.

Donny's eyelids were all twitchy. He obsessively stared at the desk beneath the tiny window, the expensive stereo, the jazz albums, the Gibson jazz guitar and Fender '65 Twin Reverb amp, and the fancy pants bookcase stuffed with brand new paperbacks.

Donny said, for at least the twentieth time, "Walker, a famous writer? That quiet, weird loner? Unbelievable! He's a Rubber Man, a big-mouth nerd, a button pusher. But a famous *author*?"

"Don't let Walker's success upset you, Donny," Norb said. "Writers aren't special. And I can say that because I'm one."

"You're definitely special, Norb," John said. "But there's a difference between writing comic books and writing *these*. He was leafing through a stack of contracts on Walker's desk. "Look at all these pen names," he said. "Daniel Paterson, Eugene Morgan, Anne Delany. All *New York Times* bestsellers! Unfuckingbelievable!"

"How rich do you think he is?" I asked, having no clue about the publishing world.

"Very," John said. He caught Donny's eye. "Looks like Walker had the right stuff, Love. Who'd have thought."

Donny's eyes had double-glazed. "*I* should have the right stuff," he muttered.

"All published by DoubleDay," Norb said, examining the spine of a book he'd pulled off the shelf. He looked at the front cover. "Wow. A million copies sold. Holy smokes!"

"Whoop-dee-doo," I grouched. "Books, shmooks. Who gives a shit?" I was pissed that Walker had eluded us—again.

Donny rifled through the desk drawers and pulled out a notebook. After a minute, his jaw hit the floor. "Oh. My. God." He blew air. "Brace yourself, Tony! You're gonna flip out!"

Yeah, right. I'd seen it all. Hadn't I?

We crowded around Donny.

John groaned. "Walker's been taking *notes* on us, too? What the fuck? Here's yours, Tone. In pink ink."

He passed the notebook to me. I read it out loud. "'Tony Valentini, a dopey blue-collar tool. Has a secret love for ballet but is afraid to tell his wife who's always in a bad mood due to her big shnoz and small tits.'"

A bomb went off inside my brain. "That lying piece-of-shit! I'm gonna fucking kill him! Angie is *not* always in a bad mood. Just sometimes. And so what if she has a big nose? She's beautiful, and he can just go fuck himself!"

"What about the ballet part?" Norb wasn't *trying* to push my buttons, but he did.

My cheeks were burning. "So, I like ballet! So friggin' what. Big deal! There, I'm out of the closet. Everyone friggin' happy now?" I was so embarrassed I didn't know which way to look. That asshole Walker had somehow overhead a conversation I'd had with Angie about us going to see the ballet! Had the prick bugged my house? More than ever, I wanted to cut off his balls and shove them down his throat.

"Ballet's cool," John said, nodding his approval. "It's the ultimate dance form. Athleticism *and* grace."

Norb struggled to read his notes out loud. His voice had peeped out to the max. The anxiety from break and entering had done a number on him. "'Norbert Reingruber marries a Scottish woman named Morag so he can cash in on her City of Hamilton pension. Secretly, he's a Nazi spy, and his comic book shop is a front for laundering money. Fun fact, Norb really did try to burn down the Dofasco mail room.'"

Norb's eyes darted back and forth like a man sitting in an electric chair waiting to be zapped. "Why would he think that? I *love* Morag. I never married her for her pension. And yeah, it's true, I committed arson—*once*. I flippin' did it, okay! But I'm not one now! I'm a changed man." He chewed off some thumbnail. "How the shamrock did Walker know that? He must have overhead me telling Morag." Tears pooled in his eyes. "Sorry I lied, guys. I'm so ashamed of myself. I worked so hard to convince myself it never happened that I believed my own lie." He started to full-out cry.

"Aw geez, Norb," I said. "Don't cry, man." I slung an arm around his shoulder and gave him a squeeze.

John passed him a tissue.

"It's OK, Norb," Donny said. "We've all made mistakes. So let the past be the past, OK?" Now, this was rich, coming from the guy who *never* let the past go, but you couldn't fault Donny because he was being so damn supportive of poor Norb. Donny took Norb's tear-stained face in both hands and planted a kiss on his forehead. Norb perked right up. It was the most tender moment I'd ever witnessed between us friends. What was happening to us? I tried not to visibly squirm. I knew how to be tender with my kids, with my wife. But this? This shit was way out of my wheelhouse.

John took the notebook next. "'John is a failed romantic and a tortured painter. His paintings are never as good as the ones he paints in his head, so he drinks alone to cope with his self-hatred. In his diary, he writes how ashamed he feels that, as a fourteen-year-old, he masturbated to a fantasy about Norbert's mom. That might be too weird or distasteful or unbelievable for a reader. Not many guys in their forties keep diaries or have sexual fantasies about their friends mommies, but still, that could make him interesting, or at least funny.'"

"What the—? What—" John spluttered. "Bullshit!" he raged on. "Norb, that's not true, OK? About Mutti." But his face went bright red. "How dare he break into my house!"

More and more, it was looking like Walker had broken into *all* our homes.

I'd wanted to tell John that we'd all had weird fantasies as teens. Reassure him. But still, that was a freaky one.

The three of us stared at each other, slack-jawed.

"I feel like Walker dismembered us," Norb said, sadly. "There's hardly anything left of us, now."

Then Donny burst out laughing.

"Yeah, laugh it up, Love," John growled. "I bet you fantasize about getting it on with your dad!"

"Jeepers!" Norb cried, horrified.

"With Dad? Have you *seen* my dad?" Donny laughed so hard tears ran down his face.

"I had a fantasy involving Angela Lansbury once," Norb offered, in a mild tone, "but I was thirteen at the time, so I'm forgiven, right?"

We all roared. Norb shrugged his shoulders.

It felt like I'd been plunging a toilet for hours and it had finally cleared.

Our stomachs ached from laughing so hard. But when John handed Walker's notes to Donny, we stopped on a dime. Whatever Walker had written—fiction or fact—was guaranteed to have a massive effect on Donny. Yes, there was a certain karma to this moment, considering the number of outrageous fibs Donny had written about other people in the past couple of years, but I still held my breath.

I hoped the letter made Donny hate Walker so much he'd finally stop looking to the past for his happiness. Then he'd finally be freed, able to become a better man for himself and his family.

Donny gathered up his nerve like he was about to jump out of a plane. "Donny Love. Failed writer. Failed musician. Almost failed husband and father. He's a charming bullshitter, and looks just like a failed writer would, like he's smart enough to be one, but when he opens his mouth— no dice. Maybe he writes a column and gets famous off the back of an old high school chum who was way smarter and actually made it as a rock star because he had real talent. His wife has all the smarts (and a super-hot ass). So, maybe like the Wizard of Oz Strawman, I'll stick a brain in Donny's head. No. Not organic. Maybe make him look like a serial killer? Or Two-Face from Batman? Haha, Donny Two-Face Love! Now we're talkin'!"

Donny lowered the notebook, hands and lower lip trembling. His face was white. "If I ever catch him looking at Allison's ass or writing a book about me, I swear I'll fucking kill him!" He whipped the notebook against the wall. It ricocheted onto the floor.

The silence was painful. Walker had effectively gutted our friend. I found myself gently patting his back.

His shoulders slumped and he muttered, "So I'm a failed writer, yeah and I know I'm not smart or talented enough to get published. So what? Big deal. Nothing new there. But at least *I* have a family that loves and needs me. All Walker has is himself."

He paused and seemed to straighten up. His voice got stronger. "Never again will I try to become famous by lying about honest, hard-working people, writing a shitty novel just so I can profit off them. I won't do what Walker's trying to do. I'm so ashamed of myself for all the Steven shit." He turned to Norb. "I owe you a huge apology. I fucked you up with all that Village Vigilante, Humpty Dumpty crap. And you kept being my friend, despite it all. I'm so sorry, Norb."

Norb gave him the sweetest smile and a big hug.

It was a powerful moment—Donny had grown up, *again*.

"I'm glad you're a failed writer," Norb said.

"Me, too," John said, "Otherwise you wouldn't have come back to us. We need you, buddy."

Norb nodded.

"Ditto," I said. "Now, can we *please* get the fuck out of Weirdsville?"

Donny stuffed Walker's notebook inside his jacket.

"That's stealing," Norb said.

"Payback," Donny said. "Besides, we've committed lots of felonies today. This barely counts."

Then I remembered. "Shit, the film reels!"

A quick search of Walker's bedroom revealed a cardboard box full of footage.

"These are *our* stories, boys!" I roared, picking up the box. "Not Walker's!"

"Damn straight!" agreed John.

Donny nodded soberly.

"We're the real deal, boys," John said, "not the bullshit fictional ones in Walker's head."

"Fucking right we're real!" I cried. But as we got to the top of the stairs, we heard a siren wailing on the street outside the house. We froze. The hairs on my neck stood actually stood up.

Norb shrieked. "Oh, my *Gaaawd!*"

"Boot!" Donny yelled, grabbing me by the arm.

We stampeded down the stairs and across the living room, then barrelled down the basement stairs and scrabbled back through the tunnel. I figured we could hop a few fences to get some distance from Walker's backyard.

Norb was making bizarre mewling sounds, and John was cussing a blue streak.

At the end of the tunnel, John, Donny and me squeezed back up through the opening, but Norb kept slipping back down into the hole, so we had to reach down and try to haul him out. On the third try, as he popped out of the hole, he lost his balance and swung backwards, taking us all with him.

We crashed against the statue of Dear Lord Steven.

We watched, in horror, as it toppled towards the house. At the last second, it veered and crashed against the fence and hit the ground with a mighty thud. The impact severed the head. It rolled towards us and stopped. Steven was smiling up at us, as if he'd just played a terrific joke on us.

We scrambled to our feet.

"We broke Steven!" Donny cried, staring at the broken statue. "Holy shit!"

"Are we going to Hell for this?" Norb asked in panic.

Donny grunted trying to pick up Steven's massive head. He barely budged it.

"Don't even think about it, Love" I warned him. "And Norb, it's just a piece of marble, not God, alright? So no, we're not going to Hell for this." Although we'd done lots of other shit tonight that was definitely tilting the scales in that direction.

"It's over, boys," Donny said, his voice cracking. "It's all fucking over." I'm no psychologist, but I'm pretty sure he was grieving a lot more than the death of his old friendship. He was grieving the death of his dreams and his youth—the whole kit and kaboodle. Only a couple of decades late.

The sirens wailed louder.

"Run!" I hissed.

We all helped hoist Norb up over the fence, trying not to groan under his weight. I hauled myself up to the top and passed the box of reels from John over to Norb. I threw Donny the keys and told him to bring my van around to the alleyway behind the house. He took off like a jack rabbit.

John took a step back, ran, leapt up and grabbed the top of the fence and vaulted right over. Gene Kelly would've given him a standing ovation, it was that beautiful.

I took the wheel from Donny and blasted us down the alleyway, then down a bunch of obscure side streets.

As an adult, I'd never been so scared *or* thrilled. Sadly, breaking and entering and stealing and fleeing a crime scene had made me feel frickin' alive. It was like playing Nicky Nine Doors, but for grown-ups. I didn't want to spoil the moment with regret or guilt.

Donny said we owed Walker for our "Fountain of Youth moment". Norb just kept giggling. John said Walker could stick the Fountain of Youth up his ass, but I noticed he couldn't stop smiling. The more I thought about what Donny had said, I began to see that he was right. This whole Walker disaster *had* made us feel young again, if only for a moment in time. But I sure as hell wasn't going to say thank you.

Epilogue

ONE YEAR LATER, A LOT has changed.

The next morning, John and Donny had gone back to John's car. There was no sign that the police had noticed it.

Weirdly, it all went away. No charges, and no more signs of Dave Walker, either.

We had no real idea why. Donny figured he'd wanted to keep us out of jail so he could keep filming us. That was the most logical reason. "But what about his notebook?" I'd asked. "He must be freaking out we have it."

"I'm sure he filmed us at his house using peephole cameras," Donny had said. "He knows we have the notebook and his films."

Then John said, "Maybe he wants to film us reading his notebook and watching his films."

Although Donny was desperate to keep them, we made the grown-up decision to destroy them without reading or watching them first. It was like pulling Donny's teeth, but he finally agreed it was a healthy decision.

Walker's publishers, past and present, responded to Donny's emails asking if he could have Walker's contact info, saying that Mr. Walker was a very private man with a strict, no-contact policy. One assistant whispered into the phone, "Think J.D. Salinger." Donny had to explain to me what that meant. Apparently, Salinger was some nutjob recluse writer who'd sold millions of copies of his book *The Catcher in the Rye*. I'd forgotten about it—on purpose. Like all the other stupid books I'd been forced to read in high school.

The day after we'd escaped Walker's house, a For Sale sign had gone up on his lawn. A year later, the house still hasn't sold. The lawn's overgrown with weeds, and the roof's missing shingles. You couldn't pay me a million bucks to go in there again or crawl through that tunnel. I can't believe we ever did that. Just thinking about that time gives me the willies.

Oh, and the next day the statue was gone. Like it had never existed.

Donny still cooks up schemes to find Walker, but every time he tells us about them, he loses his steam.

We think the reason Walker never took Donny to court for stealing his name had to do with Walker feeling sorry for him, knowing Donny didn't have the talent to get published by a legit publisher on his own merits. Either that, or Donny's Notice of Claim was lost in the mail.

Elise, who'd served us for years at Tim Hortons, died of cancer. We missed her tough, cheerful presence. Then there was the big turnover in staff. After that, Tim's just wasn't the same anymore. So, instead, we tried going to Mr. Mugs. But that place didn't feel quite right, either. We're still searching for the perfect Steeltown coffee shop.

Speaking of change, The Tartan Club sold. I didn't think that would make me sad, but it did. And Mr. Opinion himself, Archie Love, somehow beat the odds and survived. He's back at Mr. Mugs, happy to tell strangers what to think.

Once things settled down, Norb dove deep into writing Issue No.6 of *The Steeltown Avenger*. So far, no more real-life villains have targeted him, but just give it time. For such a sweet guy, he sure does have a talent for pissing off the criminal element.

Shockingly, Norb sold his Steeltown Avenger costume on Ebay for a thousand bucks! He donated the money to the Shriner's Club, except for fifty dollars which he held back for a night out on the town with Morag. Norb shyly admitted that he no longer needed the suit to make him feel courageous because he already was.

Sometimes Norb's weirdo customers show up at his shop dressed as Clint-Eastwood-Steven-Dundee, or Humpty Dumpty, and Norb happily tells them about Donny's "awesome Incognito meet-up group." Apparently, Norb's a very effective recruiter. The group has doubled in size. Don't even ask me what I think about *that*.

Oh, and Norb's a father again! He and Morag had a baby girl, Elsa. "A million-dollar family" he'd told us proudly.

John's dance studio is going gangbusters, and he's looking to rent a bigger space. Even better, Sheena's pregnant! John smiles a lot more now. It took a bit of time to get used to that. Thankfully, he can still be one sarcastic bastard when it's called for. That's his superpower, after all.

Mentally accepting Giorgio as my half-brother was tough. I'd been hard-wired to be comfortable and content with only one sister, so adding in a new blood relative after half a lifetime was almost impossible. It really helped that Angel and Angie liked him. Dad obviously did, too, and I had to acknowledge to myself that I felt a *tiny* bit jealous, sometimes. I hoped that would fade in time.

Giorgio doesn't miss racing, although he misses his track buddies, and says he's much happier doing the Lord's work. Sometimes he shows up at the raceway to cheer me on, or hangs out with me and the boys. No one had seen his career change coming, but all the years hanging out with Donny Love have taught me to expect anything, anytime, *all* the time.

In the Fall, Giorgio and Beppe invited me to go turkey hunting. I almost said no because it had never really appealed to me, but then I remembered how much Frankie loves hunting geese out west. I invited him to fly home and join us. Even though Beppe will never be one of my favourite people, we really did have a blast.

After busting her ass with work and school, Angie finally got her teaching certificate from Brock University. She just got hired to teach kindergarten at St. Anne's Catholic school on the East Mountain. She is so excited to have her own mission in life. She is going to be one hell of a teacher. Those kids are lucky.

Angel has lots of friends and seems to be doing well at school. She's forever off to soccer practice or the library. She says if she doesn't make it as a professional race car driver, she'll be a teacher, or maybe a brain surgeon, or an actress, or a foreign aid worker. I tell her that whatever it turns out to be, it'll probably be surprising, because that seems to be the way life goes.

A few weeks after my first official race at Ohsweken Raceway, the great Randy Rocket showed up with incredible news. He'd made amazing progress in his treatment. No more bandages on his eyes, his colour was good, and he was talking in full sentences. You could actually have a fairly normal conversation with the guy. His old boss had re-hired him, but only on the condition that he stay on his meds and continue to get regular counselling.

He told me his "crazy" had everything to do with the pain and guilt over abandoning three families, but he was more determined than ever to heal his broken relationships with his children, even if that meant putting up with the shitty side effects from the meds. I told him I was proud of him, which left us both pretty red-faced. I prayed he didn't go off the rails again. Shockingly, when I wished him well, he leapt up and monkey-hugged me. I hugged him back, a big deal because I'm so not a hugger. He wouldn't let go for the longest time, proof of just how much he'd been hurting.

The next day, Randy flew down to Loxley, Alabama to wrench on Jim Petty's car for the Tornado Super Sprints. After that, I only ever see him on tv, hustling around the pits like the healthy, efficient little car jockey he was born to be. I count myself blessed to have worked with such a talent.

If it wasn't for his meltdown, and John's breakdown, and Donny's half-breakdowns, I'd still be calling people "fucked in the head" or "two fries short of a Happy Meal". Witnessing their pain changed me, and that is a *great* thing. It also helped that I got a bit of counselling to deal with my own issues. It felt pretty weird at first, but Dr. Hotz is the real deal, I gotta say.

And I've gotten better at accepting that my Angel doesn't need me the way she used to. Letting go does not come easily to me. I thank God she still needs me in other ways. I'm happy we share a powerful love of sprint cars and Nascar, but I'm learning to recognize that my daughter is her own person, not a Mini Me.

Things have gotten a little better with Dad. I have appreciated the incredible effort he made to set the stage for my comeback. It really was a work of genius. And, as tough as this was for me to admit, it had been an act of deep, deep love.

At family get-togethers, we make small-talk about the weather and work and the Tiger-Cats. We both instinctively avoid topics that will lead us to butt heads. At first, my shoulder muscles knotted up with the effort to be careful, but these days I'm more relaxed.

Whenever I let myself feel some love for Dad, my heart kinda hurts but I'm working on it. These days, Angel spends more time with her Nonno. After all, he won't be around forever. When I'm tempted to feel pissed off at him all over again, I remind myself of that.

Inspired by "A Christmas Carol", which I'd finally watched straight through, I invited Beppe, Toto, Doughboy and their wives over for a pre-Christmas Dinner. It was a weird gathering, but Angie kept squeezing my hand and smiling proudly at me, so that helped. I just kept reminding myself that Ebeneezer Scrooge's lesson was one for all of us, especially me.

When they arrived in the Fleetwood—Beppe had brought it by for old time's sake—Angel asked if I she could ride in it. I said she could, but instead of creepy she'd found it cool. And I had to agree. I couldn't believe I had.

Just when we all thought life was back to normal, it delivered a final knockout blow—last month, Doubleday launched a four-book series, *The Village Idiots*. And guess who the author is? Fucking *Walker.* Yeah, he gave the characters different names, but they were clearly intended to be us.

Not that *I've* read them. Donny's been making noise about writing his *own* books about the four of us, to "set the record straight". Honestly, I wouldn't read those books, either. It's pretty clear to me that each of us just writes our own story, every damn day, by living it. Besides, who would believe some of the shit we've seen? Real life really *is* stranger than fiction.

End of story.

Would you please leave a review?

. . . .

DID YOU ENJOY *Tony Needs Speed*? If so, would you be kind enough to leave a review, either with the retailer where you purchased this book or at Goodreads? Thank you!

Indie authors rely on the kind reviews of readers to get the word out to others.

Don't miss out!

Visit the website below and you can sign up to receive emails whenever Dave Walker publishes a new book. There's no charge and no obligation.

https://books2read.com/r/B-A-CGLW-XPESG

BOOKS 2 READ

Connecting independent readers to independent writers.

About the Author

Dave lives with his writer wife, Anne L. Darling, in Hamilton, Ontario, Canada. The author may be reached at: davewalkerauthor@yahoo.com Read more at www.davewalkerauthor.com.